THE LAST CHILDREN

GUDRUN PAUSEWANG

Translated by Norman Watt

WALKER BOOKS
LONDON

First published in Germany 1983 under the title
Die letzen Kinder von Schewenborn
by Otto Maier Verlag Ravensburg
Engilsh translation first published in Canada 1988
under the title *The Last Children of Schevenborn*
by Western Producer Prairie Books
First published in Great Britain 1989 by
Julia MacRae Books

This edition published 1990
by Walker Books Ltd
87 Vauxhall Walk, London SE11 5HJ

Reprinted 1992

© 1983 Ravensburger Buchverlag Otto Maier GmbH
This English translation © 1988 Norman M. Watt

Printed and bound in Great Britain by
Cox and Wyman Ltd, Reading, Berkshire

British Library Cataloguing in Publication Data
Pausewang, Gudrun
The last children.
I. Title   II. Die Letzen Kinder von Schewenborn. English
823.'914 [J]
ISBN 0-7445-1750-8

For my son Martin
– GP

1

It didn't happen at all the way my parents and most of the other adults had imagined it would. There was no gradual build-up of threats and no declaration of war, and there certainly wasn't time for people to escape to the Alps or to some island in the Mediterranean as many had hoped.

It came very suddenly, so suddenly that it caught a lot of people in their bathing suits or lying on their deck chairs. It's true that during the weeks and days before the disaster there had been a lot of discussion about the increasing tensions between East and West. Even my mother had started to watch the TV news broadcasts, which she had never done before. But since World War II the situation had been very tense on several occasions, and nothing had ever happened.

It was the beginning of the summer holidays. No one wanted to think about unpleasant things and get all upset about them.

"Don't you think it would be better if we stayed at home for a while, till everything has calmed down?" my mother asked my father the day before we were planning to leave for our holiday. My mother had always been pretty jittery about political matters.

"That's crazy," he answered. "We might end up waiting

forever. There are always tensions; our governments will work things out all right whether we go on holiday or not. Besides, we've already told your parents that we're coming. They're really looking forward to seeing the children. You know how disappointed they'd be if we told them we weren't coming for another week or two, or maybe not at all."

So off we went, leaving our parakeet and poodle with Mrs. Kellermann, who lived in the apartment above us. For as long as I could remember she always took care of our pets and watered our plants when we went on a trip. In return we took in her cat and watered her plants when she went away.

During the trip we were in high spirits, all five of us: my older sister Judith, my younger sister Kerstin, my parents, and me. I was twelve at the time, almost thirteen. Judith was three years older, and Kerstin was only four. We were looking forward so much to spending a month in Schevenborn. We liked Bonames, the section of Frankfurt we lived in, but it would be fun to be in the country again for a while. Grandfather would be there waiting for us with his workshop and his garden on Fleyen Hill. Grandmother would be waiting too, with her home-made preserves on the big shelf in the cellar and her collection of musical boxes that she showed us every time we came to visit. My parents, as usual, were bringing her yet another musical box. This one looked like a jewel box, and when you turned the little handle it tinkled 'It's Now or Never'. My father liked to tease Grandmother about her collection, but my sisters and I thought it was fascinating. Each of us had a favourite tune.

There were lots of other things in Schevenborn that we were looking forward to: the nooks and crannies, flights of stairs and passageways between the old half-timbered houses that made perfect places for playing hide-and-seek; the massive stone tower you could climb to look out over the whole town; the castle museum that Grandfather would sometimes take us through, explaining everything in such an interesting and funny way that it never got boring for us; the swimming pool by the Scheve River, where the water was warm even on cold days. My mother was looking forward to strolling in the castle grounds; she and Grandmother liked to take evening walks all the way round the castle under the giant chestnut trees. My father was looking forward to the big forests, because he loved to go hiking, and to Lake Maldorf, where he often went fishing with Grandfather.

We took the Frankfurt–Kassel autobahn as far as Alsfeld, then turned off onto Bird Mountain. It was July and the weather was as nice as you could have asked for. My father began to sing, and we joined in; my mother sang harmony. As we drove through the village of Lanthen everything was the way it had always been.

But in the forest between Lanthen and Wietig, right at the curve in the road by Kalden Fields, there was suddenly such a glaring flash that we had to squeeze our eyes tightly shut. My mother screamed and my father hit the brakes so hard that the tyres squealed in protest. The car skidded and came to a stop sideways across the road. We were flung back and forth in our seat belts.

Just as the car stopped, we saw a brilliant light in the sky beyond the treetops. It was white and terrifying, like the light of an enormous welder's torch or a continuous flash of lightning. Although I looked at it for only a second, I was nearly blind for a long time afterwards. Intense heat rushed in through the open windows.

"What *is* that?" I heard my mother cry. She had put her hands up in front of her face. My father had his arm over his eyes. Judith, who was sitting behind my mother and, along with her, got the worst of the heat, moaned and fell sideways onto Kerstin and me.

"Shut the windows!" my father shouted.

But before anyone could reach for the handles, a raging wind came up. The trees bent over in front of us, their tops almost touching the ground. We heard the sound of cracking and splintering wood. The wind seized our car and shook it violently. We grabbed hold of each other because we were afraid we would be blown into the ditch. Judith dug her fingers into my knee. Her long hair whipped against my face. Kerstin's screams were so loud that they practically drowned out the cracking of the trees. A big pine came crashing down across the road behind us. Our car shuddered.

The wind subsided as fast as it had come. Just as it died down, everything went pitch-black, as it sometimes does before a particularly bad thunderstorm. Far beyond the woods, dark clouds were rolling in with unnatural speed. The sun disappeared. Dead calm set in.

"What is that, Klaus?" my mother cried again, grabbing my father's arm.

"Shut the windows!" he yelled, shaking off her arm so that he could turn the handle. My mother began to roll up the window on her side, too. The desperate sounds she was making really scared me. It seemed to take her forever, and even before she had the window closed another windstorm was lashing over us, this time from the opposite direction. Once more the trees creaked and splintered, once more our car started to shake. Then the air grew calm and the trees straightened up again. There was a loud, horrible roaring outside, but it didn't sound like any thunderstorm I'd ever experienced.

My father slowly turned round to us and said in a weird voice, "Thank God you're still here." Then he yelled at Kerstin to be quiet. She obeyed, which she didn't usually do. It grew still, outside and in, and Judith finally raised her head. Her face was strangely contorted as she stared out into the sombre light. I could tell by her eyes how frightened she was. But she started to laugh and couldn't stop. Her laughter turned into a shriek. I'll never forget that sound. She kept on laughing until mother shouted at her, "Stop it – right now!"

Then Judith bit into her hand. That's what she always did when she was supposed to stop laughing and couldn't. It worked. She quietened down.

We heard sirens wailing in the distance.

We all looked at each other. My mother was very pale. My father looked distraught, too, but that wasn't as easy to see because of his beard. Kerstin crawled between the bucket seats onto my mother's lap and clung to her like a monkey.

"Pull over to the side!" Mother snapped at Father. "The car's sitting across the road, for heaven's sake! What if somebody comes along?"

It was then I realised that the motor was still running. My father pulled over to the side and parked.

"Was that an explosion?" I asked.

My father nodded.

"But a whole ammunition dump must have blown up!" I exclaimed.

My father shook his head and said, "That wasn't any ammunition dump."

"Do you think –?" Mother asked Father. "You mean –?"

"It looks like it," he answered. "There's nothing else it could have been."

"But that's not possible," she moaned. "That just can't be!"

"We'll have to go back, as fast as we can," my father said. "We have to get away from here before –"

"We can't," I cried. "The tree!"

My mother sat bolt upright. "My parents! Do you think it was in Schevenborn?"

"No. Farther away. Probably in Fulda."

"Then let's drive to Schevenborn and get my parents. Come on, let's go!"

"If we can get through," he said and held his handkerchief out the window. The wind was blowing from the direction we had come from.

"If it doesn't shift, we could be in luck," he said.

"Hurry," Mother cried. "Drive as fast as you can!"

I can't say that fear was all I felt at this time, although I suspected that my parents thought an atomic bomb had exploded. The whole thing was really exciting – an adventure! Disaster was in the air. I could sense it. But it didn't occur to me for a second that it could have any effect on us.

We drove on through the forest without ever seeing any cars coming from the opposite direction. It was almost as if we were the only ones on the road.

Just before the forest came to an end, the road was blocked again by several fallen trees. But my father was able to get past anyway. As he drove over the grass with his right wheels, the birch branches scratched the finish on the other side of the car. I was surprised that he didn't get angry. He didn't even stop to look at the damage.

Above the valley where the village of Wietig was located, we had an open view of the sky. We had never seen it look so menacing before. It was dusklike and gloomy, and you couldn't see the sun. Brownish-grey billows rose in the distance. High above them, a gigantic wreath of dust and smoke spread in all directions. And looking very small beneath all this, in the hollow ahead, lay Wietig, the last village before Schevenborn.

We had to drive through very slowly. People with frightened faces ran back and forth across the street, paying no attention to traffic. They were carrying bags and bundles, dragging children along behind them, setting up hoses. Smoke poured out of a row of windows. Panes of glass had been blown in everywhere; roofs were half uncovered. A barn had collapsed and toppled onto the street. We had to make a detour around the mountain of rubble. At the end of the village we saw flames leaping out of a sawmill. Across the way, injured people in makeshift bandages were being taken to a car. A man stopped us and asked my father excitedly if the road to Lanthen was open. We told him about the pine tree that had fallen across it.

"It's probably not the only one," my father added.

"Oh, my God," said the man. "There are dead and injured people here, and the telephone isn't working –"

"Do you have any idea what's happened?" a woman shouted to us.

My father shook his head.

"Keep going," my mother said insistently. "We're only losing time!"

The last thing we heard was somebody calling out, "The road to Lanthen is blocked!" and then a lot of voices shouting. We could only make out "Schevenborn, Schevenborn," and then Wietig was behind us.

The people who lived in Wietig probably knew even less than we did, since from there you could see only part of the clouds, and the shock wave had passed over the town without causing all that much damage. The higher up we drove out of the valley, the more fallen trees we saw. The road turned into a slalom course. Sometimes we had to leave the highway altogether and drive across the fields.

"This is insane," my father said, hitting the brakes. "We're driving right into the disaster area!"

"But my parents," my mother sobbed. "What will they do?"

So he drove on.

We came to the beech forest at the top of the hill. It had withstood the storm pretty well. Then the road dipped again. We leaned forward nervously: Schevenborn lay just beyond the forest. On earlier trips we had always looked forward to the moment when we drove out of the forest and saw the town lying before us. This time we were afraid.

"There still aren't any cars coming in our direction," Judith said.

That was spooky. Somewhere, not far away, a siren was wailing loudly; we heard it clearly above the noise of the car.

Just before the edge of the forest, past a curve in the road, a tree had fallen and was blocking the way. Father had to hit the brakes hard, and Mother let out a scream. The car came to a stop only a few inches away from the tree trunk. Father pulled over to the side and we all got out. Mother took her handbag, but nothing else, since she had to look after Kerstin. My little sister didn't understand why she had to get out of the car all of a sudden, and burst into tears. Father started to lift out our two suitcases.

"Leave the suitcases in the car," Mother called. "After all, we're just going to get my parents and then drive back with them!"

"But the road is blocked!" Father answered impatiently. "And anyway, do you suppose we'd ever see them again if we left them here in the car?" He was already walking off with the suitcases, panting; at that time he was pretty fat. Mother dragged Kerstin along behind her.

We had just climbed over the tree when another car stopped in front of the barrier. I turned around and saw that it was the car with the injured people from Wietig. I heard someone groaning. A man jumped out of the car and called to us, "Can you help me, please? I've got three badly injured people in the car. They need a doctor right away. It's an emergency!"

My father hesitated, but my mother said, "We've got our own emergency, and we have three children with us!" She hissed at us, "Come on, keep walking. If we let ourselves get involved in this, we can forget about Grandma and Grandpa."

"But *I* could –" Judith began.

"Sure, that would be just great!" Mother shouted angrily. "And where would we find you when it's time to go? We're staying together. That's all there is to it!"

All of us – except for Kerstin – were accustomed to obeying our mother. And so we walked on. The man from Wietig shouted curses after us.

2

I had walked the fastest and got to the edge of the forest before the others. At first when I saw Schevenborn lying in the valley, with Castle Hill looming above the centre of town, it looked the same as always, except that a brown dusty mist hung over the roof-tops. Then I caught sight of smoke pouring out of the houses.

Judith came up behind me. "The church tower is gone," she gasped. She was right – it simply wasn't there any more. Only the old castle tower was still visible.

When Mother caught up with us, she took one quick look at the town and screamed, "Oh, God – my parents!"

Judith and I wanted to run on ahead, but Mother called out, "We have to keep together. You could run right into the fire!"

On foot, the road that led to the first houses seemed unending; we had always driven down it before. As we walked on, the scene changed before our eyes. We could see that smoke was coming from all over the town, not just one section. Flames leapt from the roof-tops, spread and grew bigger; finally the whole town disappeared under a dense cloud of black smoke. But this cloud was nothing compared to the enormous cloud we'd seen beyond Cold Mountain off towards Fulda.

Soon we saw that a lot of houses no longer had roofs. We could look right into the attics. When Judith and I stopped for a minute to wait for Father and Mother, Judith said, "Do you hear screams, Roland?"

I listened. Yes, I could hear them. People were screaming all over town. It sounded awful. But everything still seemed so unreal to me – it was as if all I had to do was wake myself up and Schevenborn would be what it always had been: a picturesque, sleepy little town with lots of flowers.

When we reached the first house we saw that part of its roof and gable wall had collapsed. A car lay half-crushed under the rubble. A dog was whimpering and a woman's voice moaned, "Bernhard, Bernhard!" Soon we were walking past fields and gardens again. The smell of fire was getting stronger all the time. We could already hear flames crackling and snapping. An old woman came down the street towards us carrying a dachshund in her arms. She had forgotten to button her blouse.

"It's the end of the world! It's the end of the world!" she cried over and over again.

"Mrs. Pakulat," my mother called out as the woman got closer, "do you know anything about my parents, the Felberts over by the South Gate?"

But the woman didn't seem to see or hear anything. Wild-eyed, she ran on down the street.

I turned to my parents and pointed towards the school. What was left looked like a skeleton. All the big windows had been blown in.

It wasn't until we got to the centre of town that we realised how bad things really were. Several half-timbered houses in Weaver Street had collapsed. Thick smoke was pouring out of Zechmeister's bakery. Window-boxes, roof tiles, even whole building fronts covered the street. Stotz's petrol station burned like a torch. A man was desperately trying to manoeuvre his car down the street. He was honking the horn crazily. The car teetered for a while over the debris and then got stuck on a pile of beams. No one paid any attention. People were frantically trying to rescue their possessions. Many were helping others who were injured. I recognised Mr. Winterberg, who was carrying his daughter Annemarie. Her head was covered in blood and her arms dangled limply. We had often played with Annemarie during the holidays. I suddenly felt sick.

As we passed the youth hostel, we heard people screaming inside. In front of the watchmaker's shop a woman lay motionless in a puddle of blood. Judith ran into Dyers' Lane to avoid going past her, but Father called her back. Then she grabbed my hand, shut her eyes tightly, and let me guide her, even though she was older than I was.

We were planning to cross over Market Square and walk down to the South Gate, but we couldn't get through. Fires blazed all around the square. The intense heat forced us to turn back. We tried to make our way along Lanthen Road, but the corner building, which housed a pharmacy on the ground floor, was on fire. The wind blew sparks to the building on the opposite side of the street, where smoke was already beginning to seep out of the roof, so we made a detour along Fulda Road. There, two roofs were on fire, but we could still get through. At the door of one of the burning buildings a woman was shouting for the fire brigade, but none of the people hurrying by paid any attention. A man came tearing past with blood streaming down his face. His hair was streaked with red. The small child he was carrying was also spattered with blood. He ran into the hospital on the corner of Fulda Road. People were crowded together there under the arched gateway and in the courtyard; some were injured themselves and some were supporting others who couldn't stand on their own.

When we finally got to our grandparents' old half-timbered house, we breathed a sigh of relief: it was still standing. A mountain of debris – pieces of mortar and roof tiles – was piled up by the front door, and all the window panes were broken. But after what we'd seen, this didn't seem all that bad. Mother leaned in an open window and called out, "Dad! Mum!" There wasn't a sound, so she ran to the back of the house and shouted through the kitchen window. I ran behind her. Nobody answered. But we heard Mrs. Kramer on the second floor, lamenting as she swept up the remains of her possessions. She was my grandparents' boarder. Mother called to her and asked if she knew where her parents were.

Mrs. Kramer leaned out of the window and shouted, "Oh, Mrs. Bennewitz! Your parents went to Fulda this morning! They weren't expecting you till this afternoon. They just wanted to run in and buy a tent for the children. There's... there was a tent sale on at Karstadt. If only something hasn't happened to them in all this..." She couldn't find a word to describe the disaster.

Mother ran to the front of the house where Father was. Kerstin was hanging onto his leg, crying noisily. The neighbour, old Mrs. Malek, had just told him, too, that our grandparents were in Fulda.

"They were planning to be back around eleven," she said and looked at her watch. She saw that it had stopped and stared at it, looking perplexed.

"It must be eleven by now," she said. "They should be back any minute."

Mother looked at Father.

"If the explosion really was in Fulda..." she murmured.

"I know," he answered.

"I have to go there," she said.

"Are you mad?" he shouted. "If it really was what we think, then there's nothing left there – and the whole place will be contaminated!"

"I'm their only child, Klaus," she insisted. "I can't just give up on them! I'll get back all right."

She was already walking off in the direction of the castle grounds. Kerstin broke into a loud wail.

"It's over twenty kilometres to Fulda," Father called after her. "You don't really think you can make it on foot, do you?"

"I'm in good shape. You know that," she called back. "Fitter than you! Stay here with the children."

And off she went. Father ran a few steps after her, then turned back. Mother really was in much better shape. Whenever they went hiking she always kept way ahead of him. He couldn't possibly catch up with her now.

"Should *I* run after her?" I asked.

But he wouldn't let me. He told us to climb into the house through the kitchen window, and then passed Kerstin in to us. She was still crying and nothing we did could quieten her down.

"Mum will be back soon," I assured her.

Judith looked at me out of the corner of her eye, as if to say: Don't lie like that! I shrugged my shoulders.

Inside our grandparents' house it looked the same as usual, except that there was broken glass lying under all the window-sills. The wind blew through the rooms and the curtains moved in the draught. A few pictures had fallen off the walls, and the coffeepot had tipped over on the kitchen counter.

"You'd better find something to eat," Father said to Judith and me. He was going over to help the Maleks; falling roof tiles had demolished their rabbit hutch and nine rabbits were hopping around on top of the piles of rubble.

Judith wasn't hungry, but Kerstin and I were. We found a jar of elderberry jam in a cupboard. That was our favourite kind. At home in Bonames we never had it. We ate almost the whole jar, without any bread. We were pretty sure that on an unusual day like this no one would be cross with us over a little bit of jam. Then we had some bread, too, with thick slices of homemade sausage. Kerstin was happy again. Once in a while she would ask where Mother was, but she didn't seem too concerned.

Fifteen minutes later Father came running in and told us to go outside straight away. A fire had broken out in the street and the wind was blowing in our direction. We ran over to the castle grounds. Judith and I each carried one of the suitcases. Kerstin took Mother's handbag, which Mother had left on the window-sill in the kitchen.

I left Judith and Kerstin with the suitcases by the castle and raced back to help Father. He had started to take all of our grandparents' belongings out of the house. Mrs. Kramer was throwing her stuff out of her window, too. There was already a big pile of mattresses, chairs, quilts, and clothing – still on the hangers – in Mrs. Kramer's flower beds behind Grandfather's workshop. We worked like crazy, dragging out one thing after another. Overhead the sky was dark with smoke, and sparks flew through the air. We heard people screaming everywhere. On the floor above us, Mrs. Kramer was sighing and sobbing, and from across the street came Mrs. Malek's tearful voice.

There wasn't time to think clearly. The fire was moving closer. Three houses on our street were already in flames. The neighbours were emptying out their houses, too. Above the South Gate, on the hill leading up to Market Square, whole streets were ablaze, and smoke rose from the new development by Oak Wood on the other side of town. Now and then there was a BOOM as tanks of heating oil exploded. Dense smoke hung over the town and slowly moved off to the east. We could hardly breathe.

For all our troubles, we did have some good luck: only one side of our roof was singed by flying sparks. Then the wind suddenly shifted. It began to blow from the north and carried the sparks back to the ruins of the houses that had already burned down. Father climbed up on the roof and put out the fire wherever it still smouldered in the rafters. On his way down he noticed that large cracks had formed in the walls. Mrs. Kramer's apartment was now a hazard to live in. The ceiling might come crashing down any minute.

The fire continued to spread to the south of our street, even though the wind died down completely towards evening. As it turned out, the last fire in Schevenborn wasn't extinguished until the next morning.

Late in the afternoon we started to carry our grandparents' belongings back into the house. Judith helped this time, but Kerstin had to stay in Grandfather's workshop; she yelled her head off because she was so angry and bored. Moving the things back was slow work, and we couldn't remember where some pieces of furniture had been. The framed photographs and vases and potted plants got all mixed up, too. When we finally had everything back inside – we hadn't been able to move the heavy pieces of furniture out in the first place – the rooms looked funny to us. And of course everything was sooty and smelled like smoke. The smell of fire was still coming in through the paneless windows, and the curtains fluttered in the breeze. Father made Judith get us some supper and then sent us off to bed. We slept in our grandparents' bed; I lay on Grandfather's side, Judith on Grandmother's, and Kerstin in the middle. The power had gone off, and in the midst of all the uncertainty we felt safer sleeping three in a bed in the darkened house. Father hardly ate anything and stayed up, waiting in the dark kitchen for Mother.

She didn't come in until very late that night. I was sleeping, and so was Kerstin. But Judith heard her coming. She woke me, and we both rushed to the kitchen, overjoyed that she was back.

In the doorway we stopped short. Some black-faced, filthy creature was clutching Father and crying loudly; it was only by her voice that we could tell it was Mother. She looked like she'd been rolling in ashes. When she heard us coming, she turned her head quickly and shouted, "Don't come in here! Go back to bed – *now!* Do you hear me?"

Her words stunned us. We went back to the bedroom, feeling confused and upset. It was a bright night. I could make out Judith's face.

"What's wrong with her?" I whispered, when we had closed the door.

Judith put her ear against the door to listen. I did, too.

For a long time all we could hear was the sound of Mother's sobbing. Father said nothing. He was waiting, we thought, until she felt ready to start talking.

"Fulda is gone," she announced suddenly.

Father still didn't say anything.

"Whether you believe it or not," we heard Mother say with her voice shaking, "everything is gone. Horas and Sickels and all the other suburbs, too – just like they'd been swept away! I climbed up to the top of a hill that looks over Fulda. All you could see was black, rolling wasteland. No trees, no buildings, just chunks of concrete here and there. They said there weren't any survivors until as far out as Glaserzell. I came across some people from Kammerzell. They looked awful: burned, maimed, blind. They were dragging themselves along the banks of the Fulda, looking for doctors, first aid stations, food, and a place to sleep. They had to stay close to the river because the villages around the city were on fire, and the woods, too, and the streets were blocked with rubble and trees and lamp-posts that had fallen over. I kept to the river, too. I saw people with burns all over their bodies. A lot of them were out of their minds with thirst. They drank water out of the river, even though it was full of ash and corpses; it must have been contaminated with radioactivity. The ones who couldn't reach the bank of the river threw themselves on the ground and sucked water from the grass. A lot of them were naked. Their clothes had been burned right off their bodies. The meadows by the river were full of corpses – in the brush along the banks, in the reeds, among the dead cows in the fields. Corpses without skin, burned corpses..."

She started to cry again. We heard Father's voice, but he spoke so softly that we couldn't understand what he was saying.

"And children's bodies," she cried. "So many children!"

Father said something again. His voice was very calm.

"But in spite of it all so many people have survived," Mother sobbed. "They can barely walk, and they're in terrible shape. I passed them on the way back. But they'll be here by tomorrow – they'll fill the whole town. You'll see for yourself what they look like...bodies without skin or hair. Don't let the children out of the house for the next few days. The shock would be too much for them."

It got very quiet. Then after a while Mother said clearly: "They're not going to come back, Klaus."

I held my breath.

"*Who's* not going to come back?" I whispered in the dark to Judith.

"Our grandparents," she whispered back.

"We might as well go home," we heard Mother say. "Tomorrow. Why wait?"

"Go home?" Father asked. "Have you forgotten about the trees on the road? We're stuck here, Inge. We'll just have to wait until the roads are passable again. Or were you thinking of walking to Bonames?"

"But what if everything here is contaminated?" Mother asked sharply.

"Then it's too late for us anyway," Father said. "And you ran right into the middle of it all..."

"You mean," Mother moaned, "there's no hope left?"

"All we can do is hope that luck was on our side," said Father. "The wind wasn't coming from Fulda, so there's some hope – even if it's small."

"You're right," Mother said. "Why would we have survived otherwise?"

Everything grew quiet in the kitchen. The living-room door creaked. I think that my parents must have slept on the rug that night, because the next morning it was grey with ash.

Judith and I groped our way back to bed and lay awake for a long time.

"But what about the people?" I whispered. "What happened to all the people who lived in Fulda? All those thousands? They can't just have disappeared."

"Why not?" Judith answered. "It's just hard to imagine."

23

"And what if everything here is contaminated?" I asked.

"From what Mother was saying," Judith said slowly, "it sounds like we'll die, too – and soon."

"Can you imagine *that* happening?"

"No," said Judith. "Not yet."

I listened a while longer to the lamenting voices that came from all over the town, and thought about my grandparents. I tried to picture them among the survivors in the meadows by the Fulda River. But I couldn't. Then I tried to imagine them dead. I couldn't visualise that either. I felt hollow, empty, dried out. My eyes were burning. I tried to swallow. My throat was parched.

"Are you asleep, Judith?" I asked.

"No," she answered. "How could I be?"

Only Kerstin was breathing peacefully. And in the kitchen, Grandmother's old wall-clock ticked away, just as it always had.

"Do you think they're dead?" I asked.

But there was no answer.

The next morning a black rain was falling. It darkened everything that wasn't already covered with soot. Mother slept until noon. Father told us not to make any noise. Once we heard her moaning. Father ran into the room. She started to flail about with her arms and scream as if she were dying. It took him a long time to calm her down. Judith put her hands over her ears. But I couldn't stand it. I ran in to Mother and cried, "What happened to Grandma and Grandpa?"

Father grabbed me and dragged me out of the room.

I tried to catch Judith's eye, but she looked right past me. For several days she avoided me. She avoided everyone. She had 'gone off the deep end', as Grandmother always used to say. The dusty light, which didn't get any brighter even in the middle of the day, filled her with dread. She couldn't bear the clouds of smoke from the forest fires; the burning odour that filled the whole town; the clammy quilts; the constant complaints of Mrs. Kramer as she moved her belongings over to her neighbours, the Mackenhausers. The lack of tap water and electricity made her fly into rages. I had never seen Judith act this way before. One day she wanted to go to Grandfather's garden. There, she hoped, the world would still be normal. But the garden was over by Fleyen Hill. She would have had to walk across the whole town to get there. When Mother told her she couldn't, Judith buried her face in Grandmother's sooty quilt and wouldn't talk or eat for the rest of the day. Kerstin was the only one she allowed to be with her; she would sit on the bed and stroke Judith's hair.

And our grandparents? No one mentioned them again, and none of us asked about them. Every once in a while neighbours or old friends of theirs would look in the window and sigh dejectedly, "I just wanted to check to see if maybe... I mean, they just might have..." Or they'd say, "Well, it's all over for them now. They're beyond suffering. They're better off than we are. Please accept our condolences."

A few days later I heard Mother say to Father, "I only hope that it was quick for them – that they were both vaporised in the same instant."

When I heard her say that, all I could picture was a drop of water sizzling on a hot stove and then disappearing. But how could people be vaporised? I brooded about it, had dreams about it. In my mind's eye my grandparents were living in a hiding place somewhere. Some day the door would open and they'd be here again, the roof would be in one piece, and Mrs. Kramer would be upstairs in her apartment. All this madness would be wiped away, just as if that bomb had never been dropped.

3

The next morning I saw the first survivors from the Fulda area stagger past our windows: ashen, bloody forms with rags hanging from them. Was it their clothing? Or was it skin? I didn't dare look any closer. First I was going to call out to Judith, but then I decided not to. It always nauseated her to see blood. I was starting to feel sick myself. When one of the refugees moaned, "Water!" right in front of the window, I fled to the kitchen at the back of the house. After a while Mother pulled the curtains across the front windows.

We survived the first few days in our grandparents' house all right, still feeling half-stunned by everything that had happened.

"Just be patient," my father consoled us. "The worst is over. Soon the emergency organisations will be arriving. They're probably clearing the roads right now so that they can get here. Until they do, we're going to have some hard times. But everything will be back to normal soon."

By that I supposed he meant connections with the rest of the world, food supplies, housing for the homeless, medical care for the injured, and so on. He had no idea that we were experiencing the last even half-way normal days just then.

They would soon be over.

Of course, he might just have been pretending that he didn't know what was in store for us. I say that because on the third day he went back to our car, which was still where we had left it, to get the rest of our things. He didn't even lock it up, although we only noticed that much later.

Now we had enough clean clothing to last three or four weeks. And for the time being, we wouldn't need to go hungry, because Grandmother had left the refrigerator and the cellar shelves well-stocked. The only problem was that the refrigerator didn't work any more. Anything that would spoil or get mouldy had to be used up as quickly as possible.

From the second day on we had no more milk, and the day after that the bread ran out. I volunteered to go into town to see if I could find any, but Mother wouldn't let me. I wasn't allowed to go anywhere except behind the house. From there all you could see were backyards. And I wanted so badly to have a look at all the destruction, especially the remains of the church tower. I wondered, too, if anyone might know what was causing this constant dusk which made the sun look so strange – like a big, blood-red disc.

Father went into town himself, hoping to find milk and bread. But none of the stores were open. Anyone who didn't have a stockpile of food was in real trouble. So many people had lost their apartments and houses! Frau Kramer, who often came over to see us, kept adding new names to the list. Most of those who lived in Schevenborn had probably found a place to stay with relatives or friends, but hungry survivors from the Fulda area were still roaming the streets. No one wanted to share the things they needed so urgently themselves with those dirty figures in ragged, singed clothing. People's questions were sounding more and more frantic: "Where are the rescue organisations? Where's the Red Cross? Why doesn't the army come and help us? Nobody's even seen a single helicopter. This isn't a place they can't get to; it's in the middle of Europe!"

It was a life full of anxiety, with no one knowing what

27

would happen next. Every day new rumours sprouted. But there was no reliable information because there weren't any newspapers, and the TVs, radios, and telephones weren't working. Even with battery-operated radios we couldn't pick up anything – there just weren't any more broadcasts. No broadcasts? That was puzzling.

"It must be atmospheric interference," Mrs. Kramer said.

"Do you suppose there's a war going on?" Mrs. Mackenhauser asked.

"Maybe it all happened by mistake," suggested Mrs. Kramer.

Every day more refugees from the Fulda area were arriving in Schevenborn. Word must have got around that the wounded were being cared for in our hospital.

"They should have closed it long ago," Father said once when he had come back from town. "It's already much too full. Conditions there are terrible."

The next day another wild rumour started to circulate: survivors from the north were supposedly in town, saying that the city of Kassel had been wiped out, too.

"Things are starting to add up," Father said. "It looks like we can forget about being rescued."

"But we have to get back to Bonames," Mother said anxiously.

Sometimes she would sit for hours now, brooding to herself and hardly even noticing when Kerstin climbed into her lap and wanted to cuddle. And Judith stayed in bed most of the time with the quilt pulled up over her head. She only got up when Father yelled at her. He had hardly ever done that before.

On the third day after the disaster, the roof and part of Mrs. Kramer's apartment collapsed. Big chunks of mortar and masonry fell out of the front wall onto the pavement.

Father had his work cut out for him now. Things had to be fixed straight away. He tried to seal the windows somehow, because the wind and rain were coming into the rooms. In Grandfather's workshop he found transparent plastic sheets that he cut to size and nailed onto the window frames. I helped him with that. After a cloudburst we noticed that rain was coming in through the bedroom ceiling. We plugged the leaks as best we could. Fortunately, Grandfather had left his workshop well-stocked with materials. But it wasn't long till we had to start locking it up at night. Someone had stolen a full container of nails out of it. Nails! They were irreplaceable.

Every day Father brought a few buckets of water up from the Scheve. It wasn't murky with ash the way the Fulda apparently was. The Scheve flows down from Bird Mountain and joins the Fulda just a few kilometres past Schevenborn, so it hadn't even come close to the charred area around Fulda. At first, though, Mother didn't want to use the river water. She was afraid it might be contaminated. She sent Father out to look for a spring or a well. He found out from local residents that there were lots of springs in the surrounding woods, but you had to hike a long way to get there. As for wells, there hadn't been any in Schevenborn for a long time, except for the one in the castle courtyard, and it was dry.

"If this area is radioactively contaminated," Father said, "then it's not only in the water. We really shouldn't be breathing the air or touching the ground, either. But how can we help doing that? The only real safeguard against contamination would have been not to come here in the first place. Maybe there hasn't been any contamination here – then we can touch and eat and drink anything we want. Or maybe *everything's* been contaminated since before we arrived. Then we can go ahead and do the same anyway, because there's no hope for us."

"Do you have to be so pessimistic?" Mother shouted irritably. She went on boiling the kitchen water in spite of what he had said.

"All you're doing by boiling the water," Father went on, "is protecting us against typhoid, maybe. We won't have much longer to wait for that. It'll be here any day now."

"Stop it, stop it!" Mother cried. "You make a person just want to give up! Didn't you say yourself that we have at least *some* chance of survival?"

There was an old coal-burning stove out in the shed next to the workshop. My grandmother had never been able to bring herself to throw it out or sell it. Father and I hauled it into the kitchen as a replacement for the electric stove. Now Mother had to learn to cook over a fire. We sawed up the charred rafters and brought them into the kitchen for firewood.

We had to use water very sparingly. Real showers or baths were out of the question. Every evening Father poured half a bucketful over me, and I did the same for him. Mother and Judith used a big basin to wash in. Then they put Kerstin in it, and after that Mother used the same water for wiping off the kitchen counter. Once we would have scoffed at such primitive ways.

Gradually the dusty light began to get clearer. The sun shone again. Wonderfully hot swimming weather followed. We thought back wistfully to the past summer, when we'd been in the pool almost every day. Now it was closed. I asked if I could go swimming in the Scheve.

"Don't tell me you want to swim in everyone's drinking and cooking water!" Father replied.

"And anyway," Mother added, "how could you possibly have a good time when there's so much misery around us?"

She was right about that.

The toilets didn't flush, of course, because the whole water system had not been working since the first day. The garage wasn't being used for anything, so Mother set a bucket out there. We emptied it on the compost heap behind the workshop. We put our rubbish there, too, since there weren't any more collections. It all began to stink, and Mrs. Kramer complained about it. But what else were we supposed to do?

Whenever Father didn't need me to help him with something, I'd sit behind the curtain in the living room and peek out. I watched the refugees filing past, begging for food and water: half-naked, miserable, desperate hordes of people. But I didn't go running to the kitchen any more to escape.

Once Mother caught me sneaking a look. I expected her to explode, but she didn't get angry at all. She stroked my hair and started to cry. That made me cry, too. She put her arm around my shoulder and led me away from the window.

"Don't let them see you," she said. "They might come to the door. We have to save the few provisions we still have for ourselves."

As soon as she'd said that I stopped crying.

"How about if it was *me* walking past out there?" I asked. "Or Kerstin?"

"It's a rotten thing to say, I know," she answered. "But I can't help out other people at *your* expense."

By the fourth day I couldn't stand staying in the house any longer. I wanted to see with my own eyes everything that Father had told us about. I asked permission, I even begged. Mother wasn't going to let me, but Father finally said to her, "Why not let him go? He's pretty tough. So far he's taken things better than the other children. They'll all have to start getting used to it, you know. And in the long run I can't do everything myself. He's twelve years old, almost thirteen. He can take over a lot of the work that you and I do now. Like hauling up the water."

He handed me a bucket and sent me down to the Scheve. I ran through the castle grounds, swinging the bucket. At one point I turned around and looked back at the town. But it wasn't the Schevenborn that I had known. It was a place full of ruins, a place without a church tower – and the beautiful summer day and the blue sky couldn't do anything to change that.

"What are you up to – stealing things?" a woman's harsh voice demanded. I was walking past her vegetable garden on the edge of the castle grounds. "Get out of here, if you know what's good for you!"

She threatened me with her spade. I didn't know the woman, so I looked around to see if she meant someone else. But I was the only one there. Then it dawned on me that she thought I was a refugee. They must have been stealing from people's gardens to keep from starving.

I scooped up a bucket of water from the river and carried it home. But then I sneaked away again as fast as I could. Anything but having to stay in the house!

There was a lot to see. The Maleks were digging around in the rubble that had been their house. It had burned down on the day of the disaster, just before the wind had shifted. Old Mrs. Malek was picking up anything that was still usable and putting it in a bag. She talked to herself the whole time. Tears were running down her cheeks. I almost didn't recognise her at first, she looked so dirty and miserable.

Mr. Malek had gone to the same school as Grandfather. He looked up and asked, "Are they still not back, Roland?"

I shook my head.

"Before they left they asked us if we wanted to go along with them," he murmured. "But we didn't have time. I wish we'd done it now."

"Don't be ungrateful," Mrs. Malek scolded him. "Good Lord, we've been lucky. We have a place to stay at Meissners' and we still have the garden. We're not going to go hungry – at least not yet."

"That's what I mean," he sighed. "It'll drag on and on."

There was a crowd of people in front of the grocery store on the corner. I looked through the store windows. Mrs. Kernmeyer was sitting at the cash register. A long line of shoppers stood waiting with their arms full to overflowing. Mr. Kernmeyer was over by the entrance, letting in groups of ten at a time.

"We're selling everything we have before the refugees ransack the place," I heard him tell someone. "I'm afraid the good times are over. Now it's dog-eat-dog, just like in '45."

"Why are we standing in line like this, anyway?" a young woman with a bandaged shoulder asked. "We don't need to go by the same rules as we used to."

Several people nodded. But no one, not even the young woman who had spoken, seemed ready to break out of the line, which continued to move gradually towards Mr. Kernmeyer.

When I came to Fulda Road, I noticed all the cars in the street. Some were buried under rubble, some were burned out, others looked like they could still be driven and were just covered with a thick layer of dust. But none of them were moving. The street had been transformed into a pedestrian zone. Most of the people I saw were carrying large cans. They were on their way to get water.

A little further on I met Mike Schubert. He was a mate of mine. I had often played with him in past summers. He was about my age.

"Boy, were you lucky!" he exclaimed. "I heard that Frankfurt was totally destroyed, too."

I stared at him, horrified. First I thought about Noppi, our poodle, then about Mrs. Kellermann, and Frank and Sandra Kellermann. Frank was Judith's age and Sandra a year older.

"See you later," Mike said. "I'm in a hurry. I have to get over to the school."

"How come?" I asked, still completely in a daze. "It's the holidays."

"My mother is helping out there. The fire brigade has set up a soup kitchen. They make food for people who've been injured or don't have a place to stay. The whole school is full, even the playground. Yesterday so many showed up that they had to put them in the town hall and the youth hostel. But there's not enough food for everybody."

"My grandparents were killed," I said.

"I know," he answered. "None of the people who worked in Fulda came back, either. A lot of people died here, too – they say over three hundred. They don't know

33

exactly, though."

Then he went on his way. After he had gone a few steps he turned around and called back, "Christoph was killed, too. Do you remember him? He was our pastor's son – we built the tree-house with him last summer. The whole family's dead, except for Elke. She's staying with us now, because she's only eight. And the Meinhards have moved into our cellar. Their house was destroyed. It's really packed at our place."

I walked on and came to the hospital. I could hardly believe what I saw through the archway. The wounded were lying in long rows on the bare ground, many naked or half-naked, with family members huddled about them. Crying children were stumbling around, trying to find parents or brothers and sisters, and parents were looking for their children. I went through the gate and stared in amazement. What I saw was horrible, but I couldn't turn my head away. A woman with a burned, puffed-up face was lying near me. Her hair was singed off, too. All that was left of one of her ears was a tiny red stump. It almost made me sick to look at it. A girl about Judith's age was lying next to the woman. The only thing she had on was a pair of jeans; there were holes burned through them here and there. Her legs had deep scratches and her pants stuck to her raw flesh. At one place you could see right down to the bone. When she saw me looking at her, she turned red and crossed her arms over her bare chest which had already begun to develop a little.

I looked away from her and out over the rows of people. Everyone was mixed together: men, women, and children, those who had been injured, burned, or had lost a limb. In most cases their skin was hanging from their bodies in shreds. Many were lying in vomit, others in blood. It stank of excrement and urine. And then there were the pathetic, pleading cries for water; they came in waves, sometimes louder, sometimes softer, then rising to uncontrollable screams.

"Hey," the girl with the mutilated legs said hoarsely, "can you bring me a little water?"

I nodded and ran home. It wasn't far. I took Grandmother's milk jug and poured the last of the water from the bucket into it.

"You'd better go and get some more water," Mother said.

"I will," I answered, "right away." I raced off with the jug before she had time to ask me what I was doing.

The girl couldn't sit up. I held the jug to her mouth and she drank in big gulps. All around us other people were begging for water now, too. They were going crazy – they pushed each other out of the way and almost tore the jug out of my hands. They weren't acting like human beings, in fact they hardly even looked human. I shared out the water until the jug was empty. Saliva, blood, and phlegm were sticking to its rim. I thought I was going to throw up.

The woman with the mutilated ear hadn't asked for water. I wondered why. I bent over her and asked, "Do you want some water, too?"

She didn't answer. She just lay there motionless with her eyes wide open.

"She doesn't need water any more," the girl said. "She's dead."

I jumped up and shouted, "Someone's died over here!"

I thought that people would come running. But no one paid any attention except for an old man lying two rows away. "It's the same over here, son," he said. "We're surrounded by dead people. She'll have to wait until the next lot gets picked up. At least there's that much order left here. Don't worry, it just takes some getting used to –"

I looked around more carefully. The man was right. A lot of the people lying there weren't moving. Some of them had twisted arms or legs. One woman was screaming and shaking her small child, who was hanging from her arm like a wet rag. A young man with a leg missing lay with his eyes closed, his face pale and bluish. The stump of his leg was poorly bandaged and blood was oozing through. A while later some men came through the rows with a stretcher, picked him up, and carried him off. They took the screaming woman's child away from her by force and laid it across the dead man's chest. The bandage slid off his stump. I could see his bloody flesh hanging in shreds.

Then I fainted.

When I came to, I was lying next to the girl. The sun was shining in my face. A woman was walking down the rows with a bucket of water, giving each person a cupful. She had to help a lot of the people who couldn't hold the cup themselves. Some of them couldn't drink properly and the water trickled out of the corners of their mouths.

But before she got to me, I jumped up and ran off, even though I was thirsty, too. As I went through the gate I recognised the men who had been picking up the dead. They were pushing a two-wheeled cart that was covered with a tarpaulin. I followed them. One of them turned around and said, "Keep away, kid, this isn't for children."

I stood where I was and gave them a little head start. Then I followed after them again at a distance. They went out to what the townspeople called the Bleaching Field, a large meadow next to the Scheve. An enormous pit had been dug there. The men grabbed the dead bodies by the arms and legs and tossed them in. I couldn't help thinking about the mother of the dead child. When the men had left with the cart, I went over to the pit and looked in. But I couldn't see much. They had strewn lime over the bodies.

When I got home I noticed that I no longer had the jug. I went looking for it, but it was gone; I couldn't find it in the hospital courtyard or at the Bleaching Field. I think it ended up in the pit with the lime.

4

From that day on I was at the hospital more than at home. Father was annoyed about that, because he needed me to help him. "Well, how about Judith?" I asked. "Why can't *she* go and get the water for a change? There's so much to do at the hospital."

At first I only wanted to take care of the girl, but soon other patients were calling out to me. And every day new ones arrived. Their friends and relatives helped them in with their last reserves of energy and then collapsed beside them.

I did whatever I could. But I still was most concerned with the girl. I filched things for her to eat from Grandmother's supplies, because the soup they dispensed three times a day at the hospital was getting thinner all the time. I brought her one of Judith's T-shirts, too. That really made her happy. Gradually she told me more and more about herself and what she'd been through.

Her name was Annette and she was the only one in her family who had survived. The Rothmanns had lived about halfway between Schevenborn and Fulda. There was a steep slope at the back of their house which had lessened the intensity of the shock wave. Annette's father and her three brothers had been killed in Fulda, and her mother and grandmother were buried under the ruins of their house. Her grandfather had been working in the garden when the blast came; although seriously injured himself, he had pulled her out from under the wreckage. He had found his wife's glasses, still in one piece, but that was all. There were virtually no other signs of life in their neighbourhood, and off towards Fulda everything looked dead and grey.

Annette had barely been able to walk because of her leg injuries and crushed chest. Her grandfather had had to pick her up and carry her every so often. He'd been hoping to find refuge on Bird Mountain, which he thought wouldn't be contaminated. But they couldn't find a bridge across the Fulda, and so they had trudged along the river, where at least there was water to quench their terrible thirst. Her grandfather had been glad when Annette began to complain that she was hungry. He took it as a sign that she wanted to live.

Passing through a destroyed village, they had picked a few early apples in an orchard. Even though they weren't ripe, they were already brown and wrinkled like baked apples; the trees dropped leaves at the slightest breeze, just as if it had been autumn. A short distance from Schevenborn a farmer's wife had given them a dried-out cake and said, "I've had this for a while, but I haven't been able to take even a bite. My daughter baked it. She never came back from Fulda."

Then they had arrived in Schevenborn and asked the way to the hospital; they'd pushed their way through the crowds of injured people who were screaming for help in the streets. Since there was no room in the hospital building itself, they'd had to find a place to lie down in the courtyard. They had almost frozen during the nights, and in the mornings they were damp with dew. Annette's grandfather could only lie on his stomach. First he'd been feverish and vomited yellow mucus; he couldn't get enough to drink. Dark spots started to appear over his whole body, and then his hair had fallen out. The last thing he had said to Annette before dying was, "Don't give up. Maybe you'll make it." Then the men had loaded him onto the cart.

I spoke to my parents. I asked them to let Annette come and stay with us, but my mother refused. She didn't want to have to face any more misery.

Annette wouldn't have been in the house for long. She grew weaker and weaker. Even when I tried to feed her she couldn't eat anything because of her constant nausea. She had diarrhoea, and towards the end she vomited blood. Her hair fell out in clumps, and the wounds on her legs got infected. She spent the last two days of her life on a mattress in the basement of the hospital. Then she was carted off, too. I walked after her. I didn't want to leave her alone.

"Stupid kid," said one of the men to me, "she's dead!"

I went along anyway. I just couldn't get used to her not needing me any more.

Rumours became more and more persistent that not only Fulda and Kassel, but all the big cities had been destroyed, and that there had been several million deaths. All my mother said to that was, "I'll believe it when I see it with my own eyes."

Father made no comment. It was obvious that he would have preferred not to believe the rumours either. But secretly he was already convinced that they were true.

Even after Annette's death I stayed on at the hospital to help. The steady stream of injured and sick people was letting up a bit. The doctors, who'd been working almost around the clock, could relax once in a while. But the Bleaching Field was completely dug up. Some people said there were twelve pits, others talked about fifteen. People from Schevenborn and outsiders were buried side by side.

"I want to be buried in the cemetery!" shrieked an old woman in the corridor of the top floor. "That's the least you can do for me if you know I'm going to die!"

She tried to bribe the men who picked up the bodies. I saw her offer them a thousand-mark note. She apparently had a lot of money with her, in her little crocodile handbag. But it was no help against the dark spots on her skin and the clumps of hair caught in her comb, certain signs of radiation sickness.

The grave-diggers simply shrugged their shoulders; none of them would take the money.

"The Bleaching Field is closer to the hospital," one of them said. "The cemetery is way over on the other side of town, up on a hill, and there are a lot of places where the roads aren't passable. Try to understand – there's just no way we can do it. We're happy if we can even half keep up. Or would you rather have your body lie around for a few days in this summer heat before it gets buried?"

"But packed in so tightly like that, next to God knows who –" the woman complained. "I'm used to better than that –"

The gravediggers were getting exasperated. They had work to do.

"All they need to do is clear the rubble off the street that leads to the cemetery!" she insisted.

Although I felt sorry for her, that seemed pretty selfish to me. As if there weren't more important things to do than clearing mountains of rubble off the streets! It was much more important, for example, to make sure that there were enough supplies to go around. Everyone was beginning to realise that much harder times were in store for us. There was nothing left to buy, and food and medicine were particularly short. Refugees had looted both the supermarkets. At first the townspeople had tried to stop them, but then they had joined in the looting themselves. Battles were fought over cases of margarine, sides of bacon, bottles of cooking oil, and chocolate bars. One refugee supposedly killed another in a fight over a chunk of cheese.

After the supermarkets, the smaller grocery stores and bakeries and butcher shops were ransacked, and finally the textile and shoe stores, the hardware stores, and toy shops. The only thing no one was interested in was electrical supplies.

I was there when the nurses and assistants cleaned out the pharmacy opposite the hospital. The pharmacist helped us, but looters grabbed the boxes, cans and little bottles out of our hands. There was a real fight, and the looters ended up with a lot of medical supplies that we thought we'd safely stashed away. We did manage to salvage a fair amount, though.

People broke into the kiosks and cigarette machines, too. Then came the petrol stations. People carried petrol home in buckets and jugs. Everyone wanted to ensure a means of escape once the roads around Schevenborn were clear again. The stealing of petrol resulted indirectly in yet another house fire in which two neighbouring houses burned down as well. One of the home-owners killed the boy who had dropped a burning cigarette butt into a puddle of petrol. No one did anything about it and the murderer was never punished.

I watched a group of young men climb through the windows of Mattheissen's bicycle shop and carry off the bicycles. Mr. Mattheissen had been killed when part of his store front collapsed, and in her agitation Mrs. Mattheissen hadn't thought to lock the bicycles away. Bicycles were especially useful now; you could even make headway around the heaps of rubble with one.

But where did people think they could go? I wondered.

Once I saw Father running past the hospital gate, out of breath. He had a sack over his shoulder. So he's been out looting, too, I thought to myself. When I got home, I saw the sack lying in the workshop. It was full of coal. Father had already gone back to get more and had taken Judith with him.

"What do we need coal for?" Mother shouted angrily. "By the time the weather gets cold we'll be long gone."

"Where will we be then?" I asked, surprised.

"Well, where do you think? Home, of course! Go on, run after your father and take over for Judith. She was so tired

41

she couldn't stop crying."

I found them in the courtyard of Arnold's Country Store. They and several other people were furiously shovelling coal into sacks. Their faces were dark with coal dust. Little black furrows lined Judith's cheeks. She wiped her face on her sleeve when she saw me coming.

"Go on home, I'll do this for you," I said to her.

And off she ran. But when we got back home with our sacks she wasn't there.

I looked everywhere. Finally it occurred to Mother that she might be over in Grandfather's garden by Fleyen Hill. And that's exactly where I found her. She was sitting on the bench in front of the little garden house, combing her long brown hair with a comb that had belonged to Grandmother. For as long as I could remember it had had its place on top of one of the cross-beams inside the house.

She hadn't heard me coming. The grass was swaying in the breeze, the trees were rustling. I heard her singing softly. That made me feel happy.

From then on Mother allowed Judith to leave the house. She went to Grandfather's garden every day, even if it was raining. Kerstin pestered Mother until she was allowed to go, too. Sometimes when I was at the hospital I would see them passing by. Judith looked neither right nor left and didn't answer if someone spoke to her. Kerstin, though, kept finding so many things to look at that she had to be dragged along against her will.

It was a real picture-book summer: day after day the sun shone and temperatures were warm – it was perfect weather for swimming or hiking. But no one dared go into the water or walk through the fields and what was left of the forests to pick wild strawberries, blueberries, or raspberries. The water in the brooks, the berries, even the whole forest could be contaminated. People who were starving did eat vegetables from the gardens, even though they knew how dangerous this could be. We sensed danger everywhere. No one trusted the peaceful scenery – we felt wary of the nature that surrounded us. In spite of that, though, most of the townspeople got their water out of the Scheve. Water was absolutely necessary; without it life wouldn't go on. But it was such an effort to walk all the way to the springs in the forest just to be quite certain that the water wasn't contaminated. It was an hour or more each way, and there was almost no one who still made the trek every day. Who had that kind of energy?

"We do boil the water, after all," people said to each other reassuringly.

The water in the hospital didn't get boiled. That would have been impossible, considering the quantities the sick and injured consumed. By this time a pipeline made out of a hose had been put in to connect the Scheve with the hospital. Someone had come up with a hand pump, too. Now all I had to do was carry the full buckets up the stairs. As soon as I got to each floor, they were practically torn right out of my hands. We could have used a lot more water-carriers, but so few people were willing to help.

Even though the patients didn't have to stay out in the courtyard any longer, the building was still overflowing. On all three storeys and in the basement they lay in cramped rows on the bare floor. There was a sickening stench everywhere, but I only noticed it when I came in from outside.

The doctors and nurses and the handful of helpers got more irritable every day. They yelled at everyone and refused to help any patient who was still able to walk and see.

"You should be over at the school," they would say. "We can only take care of the most severe cases here."

They could hardly find time to sleep, even for a few hours. Some of the helpers suddenly stopped showing up; we never saw them again. They knew that there were no authorities, no bosses, and no laws any more. Most of them had enough worries just with their own families at home. Every once in a while, though, new helpers would turn up; sometimes they'd stay for only a few hours, sometimes for days, and things would somehow keep functioning.

Lisa Bartz from the Senior Citizens' Home was a big help. Although she was already past seventy at the time, she worked tirelessly with the sick. She'd be there day and night, scurrying around the halls, never seeming to sleep. Although she couldn't carry the heavy buckets of water at her age, she was wonderful at comforting the patients.

"I think it's because she felt so sad when her son shunted her off into the old folks' home," Mrs. Kramer said when I was talking about her.

"Now I'm alive again," Lisa said to me. She sounded so cheerful, even though working in the hospital was terribly depressing, what with the constant running back and forth, the pleading and complaining, and people dying on all sides. The little bit of help that we could offer was nothing but a drop in the ocean.

I was constantly on at my mother to come to the hospital. Judith certainly could look after Kerstin. But Father answered for her: "You know very well she couldn't stand seeing what it's like there."

"Well, *I* got used to it!" I exclaimed.

"She's not over the shock yet," he said.

I was furious with my parents. I let Lisa know what I thought of them. She didn't seem surprised. She nodded and said, "You'll have to be patient with them. Before the disaster things were going so well that no one needed help from anybody. Oh, there were a few people who were in a bad way, but the government took care of them for us. So we just forgot what it meant to help other people and only thought about ourselves. Your parents, too. They grew up in cold-hearted times."

What she said made sense to me. From then on, whenever I came home late in the evening and saw Mother crying and Father trying in his clumsy way to make her feel better, I felt more sympathy for them.

The nurses and volunteers at the hospital were constantly

getting into arguments with the patients' families. The families didn't want to leave their loved ones alone; they wanted to help take care of them and give them support. But that wasn't possible because of the lack of space. Even children weren't allowed to stay with their mothers unless they were infants. Sometimes the nurses had to pull children out of their mothers' arms and put them outside. The mothers got so upset and the children always screamed. It was horrible.

Children of all ages huddled together out in the courtyard. Some cried, others looked confused and stared silently off into space. They wouldn't go hungry – the women who distributed the soup came round to them, too, and sloshed a ladle of thin broth into their bowls. Afterwards these were collected and washed in the Scheve. Otherwise, though, no one bothered about the children, no one said a kind word to them, no one helped them get over the agonised longing for their parents. When someone's father or mother died inside, no one told the child, because no one knew who belonged to whom. Nothing was organised; there were no lists of patients. No one knew anybody else's name.

Once as I was walking up and down the rows of patients distributing water, a woman tugged my shirt sleeve. I couldn't tell how old she was. I couldn't even say what she looked like, because her face was nothing but one enormous wound; her mouth was like a hole that was frayed around the edges. She wasn't able to swallow the water I gave her to drink. She was trying to tell me something, but I couldn't make out what. I had to bend close to hear her.

"My children are outside," she gasped. "I'm just about done in. My husband's dead. One is six and the other is only three. Take care of them."

"Me?" I exclaimed, taken aback. "But I'm not a woman –"

"I've tried to talk to the nurses," she went on, "but they don't have time to listen. You seem to care about people. And you're young. Don't leave them on their own, please!"

"But I don't even know them," I protested.

"Their names are Silke and Jens. Dark hair – and they're

45

both wearing red pants –" She couldn't get anything else out. She just looked at me desperately.

"All right," I said.

Half an hour later I finally could take time to go outside. I walked along the rows of children and looked for a brother and sister in red pants. Most of the children had moved back into the shade. Many of them were sleeping, some were crying or screaming, others gazed at the building in silence. One girl was taking care of her four little brothers and sisters, helping them blow their noses on leaves. Under the archway I found two emaciated little figures in red pants, though you could hardly tell the colour any more because of the dirt. The girl was sitting against the wall with her legs spread apart. The little boy was sleeping between her knees.

"Silke," I said, "your mum told me to say hello."

Silke looked up, beaming. "When is she coming?"

"Pretty soon," I said, and felt myself turning red.

She shook her brother and said, "We'd better go over by the door now."

"No," I said, "they'll just chase you away. You can wait at my house. Your mum knows that you're with me. I'll bet you're hungry, aren't you?"

I took them by the hand and started off.

"Can I come, too?" a boy of about eight shouted after me. "I'm so hungry!"

I turned around and said, "You're a big boy, you can take care of yourself."

When I got home, I went in through the back door and led the two children into the kitchen. My mother was alone in the house. She looked at the children in bewilderment. I told her in a whisper what had happened.

"Why did you make a promise you can't keep?" she asked reproachfully. But in her eyes I could see compassion for the children. They looked up at her anxiously.

"The first thing you two need is a good scrubbing!" she said a moment later and picked up the little boy.

I knew then that the children were taken care of for now.

46

I ran back over to the hospital to let their mother know. But she wasn't there. I searched through all the rooms, going up and down the rows – no doubt they had taken her to the Bleaching Field.

I ran back home. My mother had already washed the children in a basin and fed them; now she was dressing them in some of Kerstin's clothes. I was so grateful to her that I hugged and kissed her the way I used to when I was little.

5.

From that time on my mother was almost the way she used to be before the day the bomb was dropped. She came out of her silence, stopped brooding, showed an interest in the children, helped Father, and tried to find old friends. She took the children to Grandfather's garden and let them play there. She was even able to bring herself to unravel a cardigan that Grandmother had knitted for Grandfather, so that she would have the wool to make little jackets for Silke and Jens. Her attitude brought about a change in Judith, too, who began to devote herself to the children and often spent the whole day doing things with them.

I sensed that Father was able to relax a bit. He didn't need to make all the decisions alone any more. Having to do that had been hard on him, since Mother had always done most of the decision-making in our family.

I even got her to come and have a look at the hospital. She felt nauseated in the rooms inside. But all the children in the courtyard affected her even more, to the point that she felt she had to do something. She immediately talked two old friends from school into helping her. She found someone to blast open the portal of the castle, which had stood empty since the bombing. She and her friends swept and shovelled up the broken glass and debris from the stuccoed ceilings in the entrance hall and on the staircases. They quartered the children in the large cellar room; its windows hadn't been damaged, since they were below ground level. On the second day Mother was already taking care of over a hundred children, all under the age of ten. Besides those from the hospital courtyard, she took in children without parents who did nothing but wander through the town begging – and there were lots of them. By the third day a hundred and thirty children were living in the castle cellar. They slept on hay that Mother had found in the loft of a nearby barn. The children had to carry it over to the castle themselves. There was an enormous amount of work to be done, including transporting food. Every child had to take some responsibility.

Mother now spent almost all of her time in the castle. Judith and the three little ones were there as well. Judith couldn't do enough to help. The only thing she and Mother talked about any more were 'the children'. They tried to get me to help out in the castle, too. But I didn't feel I could do that. The hospital was filled with so much misery that no one wanted to help there. I couldn't just stop showing up.

Those were terrible days at the hospital. The building was full of the severely ill and dying, and the places of those who died were filled immediately by new patients brought from the Fulda area. Most of them were suffering from radiation sickness, the first sign of which was an unquenchable, maddening thirst. I had seen a lot of that. The next stage was nausea, diarrhoea, and high fever. Their hair fell out in clumps, their teeth loosened, and they vomited blood. Dark spots spread across their bodies. Soon it became difficult for them to swallow, their hearts stopped functioning normally, and their mucous membranes began to bleed. During the final stages the patient would babble nonsense, then lose consciousness and die. In some cases they went quickly, in others the torment dragged on and on. But in almost every instance it was clear that death was inevitable. And the closer the person had been to the blast, the more violent the symptoms were.

The only townspeople badly affected were those who had been on the way to or from Fulda on that terrible morning, or who had stayed in the area around the city shortly after the explosion. I heard the nurses and doctors talking about this and started to feel afraid for my mother. And when I heard about a couple from Hamburg who had been on holiday in Schevenborn and were suffering from radiation sickness, I felt even more afraid; they had looked into the fireball over Fulda during a hike on Cold Mountain. But I wasn't just worried about Mother – Judith must have got her share of radiation as well. She had been sitting behind Mother on the side of the car facing the blast. I had been on the left, behind Father, so she had given me cover. But I had looked into that harsh light for a split second, too. Did that mean –?

Strangely enough, this uncertainty didn't bother me a lot. I didn't have much time to spend thinking about myself. But I never stopped feeling amazed at how lucky the people of Schevenborn had been: from their valley they hadn't been able to see the fireball. And a strong west wind had driven the radioactive cloud of ash from Fulda off to the east. They might have a good chance of survival. But how about Mother? and Judith? I tried to visualise them lying with the other sick people in the hospital. It made me shudder. Then, once, in the middle of the night, it occurred to me that Schevenborn must be east of some totally destroyed city or other, and that the west wind could have blown radioactive fall-out towards us without our even suspecting it. I grew cold with fear. Hadn't the wind suddenly shifted when our roof had caught fire? Had it maybe shifted *before* the cloud from Giessen or Koblenz or some other city had reached us? But, then, couldn't the north wind have been carrying disaster, too?

I got worried when Mother started to have diarrhoea, and

even more when Judith came down with a fever. But back then everyone had diarrhoea at one time or another, and Judith had always had lots of fevers. From the time she was a little girl she used to get a slight temperature whenever she was excited about something. But how about the thirst she had all the time? Was *that* possibly the sign? The days were so hot, though, and she was on her feet from morning till night. So was it surprising that she was always thirsty?

Since the disaster the days had seemed twice as long – every day an eternity. It seemed as if the bomb had gone off years ago. And yet it had only been three weeks. During that time my thirteenth birthday came around.

My father forgot about it, probably because he was so preoccupied with getting the roof fixed. He went from one pile of debris to another, looking for roofing paper and nails. He wanted to have the roof good and tight before the autumn rains came. The fair weather wouldn't last forever. The only protection we had against rain was our ceiling and Mrs. Kramer's half-destroyed apartment above that. Father had taken on a very difficult job. Before he could put the roofing paper in place, he had to knock down the remains of the second-storey walls, saw off the studs, and shovel and cart away all the rubble.

Mother didn't forget my birthday. But she had no time to arrange anything special. She just hugged me and gave me a kiss on the forehead.

"My birthday wish is for you to survive," she said.

Before the blast I had wanted a new bicycle for my birthday. Now I was amazed when I thought about having made that wish. Wasn't it strange, all the things people used to wish for – and actually got? But I didn't go completely without presents: Judith wove me a little garland out of strawflowers she had found in the garden house. Grandmother had always grown strawflowers in her garden and dried them inside, so that she'd have bright bouquets during the winter. Before, I would hardly have taken any notice of a garland of flowers, or I would have thought: what's that good for? But now I was delighted. I still have it, although it's pretty much fallen to pieces.

Judith had told the other children about my birthday. Silke recited a poem that Judith thought up. I can only remember the last two lines now:

"Be full of cheer, whatever you do,
    And things won't get the better of you!"

Kerstin gave me a set of chequers. She had found the board under a pile of rubble and then, apparently at Judith's suggestion, had looked for twelve dark stones and twelve light ones to go with it. I thought to myself: when will I ever have time again to sit down and play a game? Playing games suddenly seemed so childish to me. But of course I didn't tell Kerstin that. She had only wanted to do something nice for me.

I picked her up and gave her a big hug. I noticed that she wasn't nearly as chubby as she used to be. Everything and everyone had changed. Even Father didn't have his pot belly any more, and his beard was growing ragged.

And then there was Jens. He gave me something that he had found, too. He hadn't shown it to anyone and had made a big secret of it. He'd even wrapped it himself, in an old piece of newspaper. It was a set of yellowing false teeth.

I was so touched by my little foster brother's good intentions that I picked him up and swung him around in the air.

Then I had to run back to the hospital; the patients would be begging for water again. I had asked Mike to help me, but he only lasted for two days. I suppose the work got too strenuous for him. Now I was on my own again, sweating over the heavy buckets of water.

Late that evening I crept in through the back door and flung myself, dead tired, on to Grandmother's sofa in the living room. Judith came in; it was midsummer and still light outside, so I could see her face clearly. She sat down next to me on the edge of the sofa, holding a comb in her hand. It was one she had brought from home. In the twilight I was struck again by how pretty Judith was; she had Mother's high forehead and Father's narrow, straight nose. Her eyes were bright blue with long, dark lashes. But the most beautiful thing about her was her hair.

"Well?" I said impatiently.

She still didn't say a word. She just raised her hand and drew the comb through her hair. When she held it out in front of her I could see that dozens of strands were caught in its teeth. She pulled them out and laid them on the velvet armrest. She ran the comb through a second time, and another tuft of her brown, shimmering hair came out.

I knew what that meant and looked at her in horror.

"Does Mum know?" I asked.

"You're the only one," she answered. "Don't tell anyone else. They'll start to notice soon enough."

So my fears had been real. Nevertheless, it came as a terrible shock. I had seen many patients who had lost their hair, but this was my sister! I didn't realise until that moment how much I cared about her.

"Maybe it's not even related to that," I forced myself to say. "Maybe it's from not eating properly –"

I saw her smile. She knew exactly what was going on and she had given up hope.

"Run your hand through it just once," she said, "so you'll be able to tell people later how beautiful it was."

She held her long tresses out to me and I stroked them. Then she went into her room. It was her night off; Mother was sleeping in the castle with the children. But I was certain that Judith didn't sleep that night. As my glance fell on the strands of hair still lying there on the armrest, I couldn't control myself any longer. I pressed my face into the cushion and cried.

The next day I happened to be in the house as Kerstin was dogging Judith's footsteps and making a pest of herself. When Judith wouldn't turn around, Kerstin pulled her hair.

Judith spun around in a rage. Kerstin let go, but several strands of hair were left in her hand. Judith grabbed them from her and stuffed them into her pants pocket as quickly as she could. Kerstin looked up at her out of the corner of her eye, knowing she had done something wrong, and was surprised when Judith didn't yell at her.

6

What everyone had been expecting and fearing happened two weeks after the explosion: the first cases of typhoid fever broke out. For a while people tried to make light of it; if a family member showed the symptoms they said it was something else. And lots of people simply didn't know they were dealing with typhoid. Who had ever had any experience of it, after all? High fever and diarrhoea could just as well come from a bad case of intestinal flu or radiation sickness.

But now, a few days after my birthday, the epidemic was spreading like wildfire. There were typhoid victims in every house. It was pointless to take them to the hospital, since it was already overcrowded and all the medical supplies were gone. Besides, the doctors couldn't handle any additional patients. Before the disaster there had been six doctors in Schevenborn. One had been on holiday at the time and never returned. Another had apparently died on the way to Fulda, and a third had been killed by falling debris in front of a patient's house. And now two of the remaining three came down with typhoid within a few days of each other. One died; the other was in such a weakened condition after his illness that for weeks he couldn't even get out of bed.

The third continued his work alone, but by that time there wasn't much he could do. Since he had no more medications, bandages or disinfectants, he had to leave the sick to their own devices. I saw him walking down the rows a few times, nodding in his friendly way to the patients on both sides. But he never paused, as he used to, to listen to their troubles, or tried to console them. One day he was found dead in the laundry room.

For a second time the townspeople began to hope for help from outside. There were rumours that a Red Cross convoy carrying typhoid specialists was on its way to Schevenborn.

"Well, finally!" I heard Mrs. Kramer exclaim. "I mean, Germany isn't an island! Don't people from other countries owe us some help? Didn't we donate millions for the earthquake victims in Italy? Don't we send thousands of packages to Poland?"

"Maybe things don't look any different in Poland now than they do here," my father replied. "Maybe there isn't an Italy any more. Maybe all of Europe was destroyed."

Mrs. Kramer called him a defeatist.

Someone even claimed to have seen a helicopter – this news sent tremors of excitement through the town. But when no convoy arrived and the helicopter failed to appear, people lost all hope; along with it, the last semblance of order disappeared from Schevenborn. No one made soup for the sick, the orphans and the homeless. They were left to fend for themselves. No one wanted to bother burying the dead, although the second great wave of dying had already begun.

The last few nurses and assistants stopped coming to the hospital. Everyone was trying to avoid dangerous situations. Those who could still walk or even crawl left the hospital, since it now contained more dead than living. Townspeople and refugees alike rushed headlong into the forests and camped out in tents, hoping to escape the typhoid epidemic that way. But many of them had already become infected;

it wasn't long before they came down with the disease and began to infect the others. I never saw Mike Schubert again. I heard later that he had died in Schornberg Forest; it was north of Schevenborn and hadn't been touched by the fires. We had often gone mushroom-hunting there together.

Those who stayed in town didn't dare go outside for fear of becoming infected. Any door handle, any railing, could transmit the disease. An encounter with a person on the street could mean the greatest danger. During the day the town was lifeless, although it had almost twice as many inhabitants now as before. But during the night the streets came alive. People would sneak off with their buckets to dip water out of the Scheve, or they'd go to the fire brigade's ponds by the city wall or the fish ponds behind the castle grounds. They were careful to keep their distance from each other while they were doing this. Bits of news were called back and forth and almost always concerned someone's death. And all of this took place in the dark; it was almost as if people thought that the sun was the source of infection.

"That's ridiculous," said my father, who went for our water during the day. He got it from the public swimming pool, even though lots of people had gone swimming there before the explosion and the water hadn't been changed since. Leaves and ash floated on the surface, but at least the water was chlorinated; my father still believed that this was the best protection. Word got around and soon every night people were crowding through the gate, which had been broken open at some point. When Father and I came in the morning with our buckets, the water level would be lower in each of the three pools. Before long the children's wading pool was completely empty. The water in the non-swimmer's pool was down to knee-deep, but no one wanted the rest because of the two bodies floating in it. No one fished them out. People pretended that they didn't notice and dipped their water out of the big pool. Not even family members bothered about the bodies; maybe they didn't have any family left.

My mother and Judith wouldn't interrupt their work at the castle even when typhoid broke out there. But they began to panic because they didn't know how they would continue to feed the children. Father had to go out to the fields and steal potatoes, although it wasn't time to harvest them yet. They weren't much bigger than marbles; he couldn't dig them out of the ground fast enough to keep the children fed. But when Mother began to use some of our grandparents' supplies to feed them, she and Father got into a fight.

"And what are *we* supposed to eat when winter comes?" he asked.

"Do you expect me just to watch while those children starve?" she said angrily.

I was amazed. Only a few weeks ago she had pulled me away from the window as the refugees came hobbling past. She had refused to give them anything when they begged for food. How she had changed in this short time! And Father had changed, too: he had become tougher and less considerate. But that didn't get him anywhere with Mother.

"Well, how about the hospital?" he cried. "Dozens of people are starving and dying from diseases over there. Why don't you feed them, too?"

"It's *children* I'm talking about," she replied.

"You've taken on too much!" he shouted. "You're trying to do the impossible. We have to draw the line somewhere!"

"But not just around our family. I can't do that!"

"Don't we have it hard enough already, now that we've taken on these two other kids? We're going to need an awful lot of luck to make it through the winter if we have to feed ourselves and them, too!"

"Well, try imagining how it would be the other way round," she exclaimed. "Suppose you and I were dead, and Judith and Roland, too. Kerstin's the only one left, and she's over at the hospital with the other children. Nobody knows her, nobody cares. How would you like that?"

Father went back out to the fields without answering. He didn't need to supply such large quantities of potatoes for long, though; the children began dying one by one. Soon he had to dig a pit on the castle grounds for all the dead bodies.

Father insisted that Kerstin stay in the house, and Mother agreed. He wanted Judith and me to stay home, too. He was scared out of his wits for us. He threatened to lock me in if I refused to stay voluntarily. I was mad at him. I wasn't a child any more and I didn't want to be treated like one. I had my responsibilities!

"If I'm going to get sick, the disease is already in my body, and there's nothing anyone can do!" I shouted, enraged. "If you try to keep me here, I'll just stay over at the hospital and never come back!"

Judith wouldn't give in either. She said calmly, "If Mother keeps working, I will, too. She can't do it alone."

"And what if you get infected?" Father yelled. "You could die!"

All she said to that was, "So what?"

I glanced at her hair. It had become thin and lost its lustre. She didn't comb it any more. Hadn't my parents noticed? Didn't they find it odd that she was drinking so much water? Couldn't they see how pale and miserable she looked? But they looked that way themselves. It was as if we were all holding our breath: we shut our eyes to what was happening because we didn't want to accept it.

When the number of neglected corpses became so great that the whole town reeked, a few of the men who had survived the fever got together and stacked up the bodies in various sections of town, then drenched the piles with petrol and set them on fire. Some people still had petrol, and cigarette lighters and matches weren't hard to come by.

The men made their rounds in the hospital as well. I knew one of them, a young man named Dreesen. He had been a photographer and owned the most beautiful sports car in town. The girls had been wild about him. Now he was helping to pile up bodies on the grassy area behind the hospital, out of sight of the patients. The stench of burnt flesh hung over us for weeks.

By now Lisa and I were the only ones left to take care of the remaining patients. There weren't very many; those who hadn't died of burns, radiation sickness or typhoid had starved to death. The few still in the hospital had no family left; they were completely alone. Whenever I stepped into one of those filthy, stinking chambers of death, the patients who were still conscious looked at me hopefully. But I had no hope for them. Those who could make themselves heard got an answer; those who couldn't weren't even given a glance. I was just about done in myself and simply didn't have the energy. The only thing I could offer them was water to quench their terrible thirst.

By the time they died, most of them had become nothing more than skeletons covered with skin. In their panicky fear of death, they grabbed my arms or my dirty, sweat-soaked shirt. Some held onto my water bucket with all their remaining energy or bit into the plastic water cup and wouldn't let go. Strange as it may seem, I had to defend myself with my fists against the dying; I had to pry their clawing fingers from my shirt. And I was already so exhausted! Once in a while I would get really scared. Sometimes it seemed as if they were trying to kill me – did they think they could live on by taking my life for themselves? And yet, I was the only one left to help them, besides Lisa, who took over now and then so I could get some sleep.

I tried to treat the patients equally and always visited them in the same order, floor by floor, room by room. It often happened that a patient who had been particularly out of control during one of my rounds would be dead by the next, staring at the ceiling with glassy eyes.

One hot afternoon I collapsed in the basement of the hospital with a high fever. Lisa found me and went for my father, who came and carried me home. During the next few days almost the whole family got sick. Only Judith was spared. I lay on Grandmother's sofa for over two weeks, hovering between life and death. Several times my temperature climbed so high that I lost consciousness, but it would drop back to normal within a few minutes.

It was only in the periods when my fever was down that I was aware of what was going on around me. I never saw Father, Mother or the little ones. But Judith was there all the time, seeing to my needs. Whenever she bent over me she would give me a sad smile. She had got thinner, and her eyes seemed to lie even deeper in their sockets. She held a cup to my lips just as I had done for the sick people in the hospital. At times I was so weak that I couldn't say a word. Once I felt my temperature rising and everything started to go black; I pulled at Judith's sleeve and held onto her hand. Another time I was about to ask why she was wearing a scarf around her head, but immediately forgot what I was going to say. Judith washed me, she changed my bedding, she made tea. I heard her bringing in buckets of water and chopping wood. The fire crackled in the kitchen stove.

I asked her once why it was so quiet in the house.

"Everyone's asleep," she answered. "You should try to sleep, too."

And obediently I fell asleep, exhausted from the few words I'd spoken. Later she told me that I had lain there for a whole day looking as if I were dead.

As soon as I was feeling a bit better, Judith told me that Kerstin, my bouncy, whiny little sister with the auburn curls, had died. She had been sick for only three days. Silke hadn't survived the fever either. Father and Mother were lying in the next room, seriously ill. They didn't know yet that the girls had died. Jens was the only one back on his feet; he'd had nothing more than a brush with typhoid – a mild case of diarrhoea. I could hear him out in the backyard, laughing with delight.

"I didn't have it at all," Judith said. "I'm destined for something else."

She asked me to tell our parents about Kerstin and Silke; she didn't have the heart to do it. But it took a few days before I was able to drag myself into their bedroom. For a minute I didn't recognise them, and they were just as startled when they saw me. We were all reduced to skin and bone. They smiled at me weakly. When I choked out what I had come to say, Mother screamed and clung to Father. He didn't say a word at first, but his eyes filled with tears. Then he looked at Mother and said, "They're better off where they are. Who knows what we still have to go through."

"Oh, you and your clichés!" Mother sobbed. Then she called to Judith. She must have been listening at the door, because just as I turned to go and get her, she came into the room. She was very pale and looked unsteady on her feet.

"What did you...do with them?" Mother asked, in a strange, shrill voice.

"I buried them behind the workshop during the night, next to the compost heap," Judith said. "I didn't want the men to take them. But the grave isn't very deep. I just didn't have the strength –"

"Oh, thank God!" Mother murmured. "They're safe under the earth."

It wasn't until later that she asked what had happened to the children at the castle.

"I don't know," Judith answered. "I couldn't take care of all of you and them, too. I just opened the door for them and said, "You can leave if you want to. There's no one here any more who can feed you. Go out to the fields and look for seeds, chew on ears of corn, dig up potatoes. Go into the woods and try to find some mushrooms. Take anything you can from the gardens. Some of the children went, but most of them stayed. They must have been hoping that we would come back. I haven't been there since. I'm afraid of what I'd find – so many of them were sick."

On the evening of the day when Mother got out of bed for the first time, Judith had to go and lie down. She had a high fever. Her jeans would barely stay up over her hips. She couldn't eat anything, but she was terribly thirsty. Swallowing got harder for her every day. Once her scarf slid off her head; her hair was completely gone. I let out a cry and in the same moment regretted having done it because I saw how much I had hurt her.

Her body grew pale and spotted, and then she died – quietly, without complaint. She simply slipped away.

Her death hit Father hard. He had been so proud of her. She had always brought home such good marks, much better than mine. Teachers would congratulate him for having such a bright daughter. I was the lazy one, the dunce, who often embarrassed him and just barely made it from one class to the next.

None of us had enough strength to dig a grave for Judith. We had to give her to the men who went up and down the streets calling out, "Any bodies? Any bodies?" But before they came into the house, Mother quickly tied a scarf around Judith's head; she didn't want anyone to see her with no hair. Then she slowly dragged herself back to the bedroom to be with Father. I was left alone with Judith and had to watch the men toss her, not very gently, onto the stretcher and carry her away.

"Why don't you take off her running shoes?" one of the men suggested. "It would be a shame to burn them, they're so hard to find these days. You'd surely be able to use them."

I shook my head.

"Then *I'll* take them," the other man said. "My nephew could use them, if he's still alive."

Before he had time to do it, I tore them off Judith's feet and threw them behind me into the room.

"Hey," the man said, "don't get violent. In times like these nobody can afford to be sentimental. If you aren't practical, you'll never make it."

As soon as they were gone, I began to feel weak and broke out in a sweat. I slammed the door behind them and didn't even look out the window. I threw myself onto the sofa and cried until Jens, worried about my outburst of sadness, stroked my neck gently and told me that he was hungry.

7

Father and Mother recovered faster than I did – at least physically, even though Mother didn't have much will to get better. She was having a hard time getting over the deaths of the girls. She withdrew into herself just as she had in the first days after the explosion; she didn't ask about anything and didn't want to hear anything. She stayed inside and wouldn't even go over to the castle. The only people she took an interest in were Father and Jens and me.

It was reassuring to see how attached she was to Jens – just as he was to her.

"He's an ideal child for times like these," Father commented once.

He really was; he always came bouncing back and never let anything get him down. He missed Kerstin and Silke for only a little while, then quickly regained his high spirits. He beamed all the time and was content with everything. Whenever we spent time with him, we were able to forget for a while all the terrible things we had experienced, and he distracted us from thinking about what we still had to go through. For him, the life we were leading was normal, and had been for a long time. He took things as they came. It was only in the night that he sometimes called out pitifully for Silke or his mother.

It took me longer than the others before I ventured outside on my still wobbly legs. Father said that I looked like a ghost. It wasn't until the beginning of September that I managed to make my way unsteadily over to the hospital.

It was empty. The rooms echoed. There was still dried blood, excrement and vomit on the floors, but the dead bodies had been taken away. I looked for old Lisa; I was absolutely sure she would be there and had been looking forward to seeing her. The possibility that she might have died was unimaginable to me. Later on, I asked some of the townspeople about her. But no one had seen her after the typhoid epidemic.

In one of the rooms in the basement I found a dirty little teddy bear, which I took along with me for Jens. I barely had enough energy to get back home. Drenched with sweat, I fell onto Grandmother's sofa.

The next time I ventured out I headed into town. It had grown very quiet there, even though the people who had fled to the forest had long since come back – those who had survived the epidemic, that is. Father told me that there was hardly a family who hadn't lost someone. A second epidemic had gone around, too – some kind of dysentery that had caused just about as many deaths as the first.

"They say that three to four thousand people altogether have been buried in Schevenborn by now," my father said. "That's not counting the people from here who were killed in Fulda."

The town had had about five thousand inhabitants before the explosion, and almost that many homeless from the Fulda area had found refuge here since then.

"That's not so bad," said old Mr. Malek, whose wife had died of typhoid. "Now there's more food for us survivors."

I looked at him with such a horrified expression that he added in surprise, "Well? That's the way it is, isn't it?"

He wasn't the only one who had that attitude. People's thoughts began to focus solely on food. It was true of us, too. Autumn wasn't far away, and the days were getting shorter and cooler. Everyone was afraid of the approaching winter.

In the first week after the explosion and during the epidemic that followed, hardly any farmers had harvested their crops. In many fields the overripe grains of wheat had already fallen to the ground, or the stalks had been beaten down by wind and rain storms and lay there in tangled masses. The townspeople went out in droves to gather up kernels. We set out with plastic bags and Grandmother's old canvas sack to do the same.

That was the first time I had gone out to the fields after my illness. I could scarcely believe my eyes: it was only September, and yet everything was withered and yellow, and the leaves were falling. Whole stands of trees were already completely bare.

"Why is that, Dad?" I asked uneasily.

"It's been so dry," he answered. "It's hardly rained all summer. When that happens, autumn comes earlier."

"But look at the turnip leaves," I said. "They're all limp. And the alders along the Scheve are already bare; they don't usually lose their leaves until November. How do you explain that?"

"You sound like a farm expert, or a forest ranger," Father said, annoyed. He grabbed me by the arm to make me stop walking. When Mother and Jens were a few steps ahead of us, he whispered to me, "*Of course* it's not because it's autumn – I know that as well as you do. But keep your mouth shut about these things when your mother's around. Otherwise she'll get even more depressed."

"So the cloud from Fulda *did* pass over us?" I asked in alarm.

"Not the one from Fulda," Father replied. "After so many atomic explosions the atmosphere over the whole country must be radioactively contaminated. It would be ridiculous to assume that exactly where we happen to be the air somehow stayed pure."

"But then all the plants are contaminated," I whispered in horror. "We shouldn't be touching anything that's growing here, should we?"

"If we don't, we starve," Father answered. "In the final analysis it doesn't matter how we die. As long as we're hungry, we'll clutch at whatever's edible, even if it's contaminated."

I didn't eat anything else that day, or the next day, either. But by the day after that I was so hungry that I couldn't control myself any longer and wolfed down the potatoes that Father had brought back from the fields a few days before.

The farmers who were still able to harvest their crops had a problem: the combines were useless now. They had to harvest their grain with scythes. Many of the younger ones had never learned how. Now all of a sudden it was the old farmers whose advice and skill were in demand. It was almost impossible to come up with a scythe, though. Some of the farmers pulled the stalks out with their hands, others cut them down with sickles or knives. But it was slow work: more workers had to be found. There were actually enough of them, except that no one wanted to be paid in money. What was money good for if you couldn't buy anything with it? People would only work for grain.

But hand threshing was hardly worth it. About all the farmers got was straw. The wheat ended up among the stubble on the ground; in fact, a lot had already sprouted. We made our way through the fields on our knees and gathered up what we could, and we weren't the only ones. The fields were teeming with grain hunters. Some of them still believed that they would find more kernels in the stalks than on the ground, so they spread out pieces of cloth on the edges of the fields, piled up the stalks on them, and beat the grain out with sticks and stones.

"Just like in the Stone Age," my father said.

"What about next year?" I asked. "These fields were all

planted before the bomb went off."

"Next year is so far away," he replied. "Let's not lose any sleep over that now."

As for the cornfields, no farmer had to bother harvesting them, at least not the ears. They had long since been picked clean by all the hungry townspeople whose provisions had run out.

There was a big crop of fruit that year. The trees in Grandfather's garden were bent over by the weight, but the fruit itself was small and strangely wrinkled. We picked the apples and pears from the bare branches and shook down the plums, but since we didn't have any sugar, we couldn't preserve the fruit. We tried drying the plums, but that didn't work; they started to get mouldy. Grandmother's experiences during and after the last war would really have come in handy!

We cut up the apples and pears in thin slices and put them on boards and baking sheets in the sun to dry. We hunted for mushrooms and dried what we found. There weren't any hazelnuts or walnuts, though; people had stolen them from the bushes and trees in Grandfather's garden while they were still green. The pumpkins, too – enormous ones – had disappeared before they'd had a chance to get ripe.

My mother's hands had become rough and cracked from all the work, and she didn't bother to take care of them any more; she always used to wear rubber gloves when she worked in the garden before. And in the morning we no longer saw her putting on make-up at her dressing-table mirror with jars of cream and powder boxes in front of her. Her face was brown from so much sun and lined with little wrinkles. She let her hair get straggly, smelled sweaty, and often had dirt stuck to her shoes. But I didn't love her any less this way; I loved her even more.

For several days Mother's eyes had been red from crying. Father looked troubled, too.

"Mother is pregnant," he said.

I stared at him in dismay. He raised his shoulders in a gesture of resignation and looked very unhappy.

"You could be wrong," I said, thinking about what we had learned in sex education class. "Maybe it hasn't come because she's been so agitated –"

"That's what we were hoping, too," Father replied. He talked to me as if I were an adult. "But it's pretty clear now that she's pregnant – and that the baby was conceived before the bomb was dropped."

"Oh, my God," Mother sobbed.

Once I had regained my strength I started to take long hikes beyond the town. I discovered that Wietig and Murn had suffered the least damage of all the nearby villages. Wietig was the farthest away from Fulda, and Murn was located in a deep, narrow valley. But there was almost nothing left of the villages in the Fulda River valley. The farmhouses had collapsed or burned down; the barns and sheds were as good as blown away. The odour of ash still hung in the air. I saw hardly any people; the survivors who hadn't left were existing as best they could in the ruins. The withered meadows were strewn with carcasses of cattle; sometimes only skeletons were left. But there was not a crow to be seen.

On the forest slopes, the shock wave had knocked the pine trees over like matchsticks, and the farther I went upstream along the Fulda, the more woods I saw that had been completely mowed down. In a pond I saw dead fish floating belly-up on the water. They couldn't have died until long after the explosion. And everywhere, especially under trees, I stepped on tiny bird skeletons.

Near a small village the road crossed over the river. There was almost nothing left of the village itself, but the bridge was still intact. A power-line pole had fallen over it, and wires hung down in shreds. I stood on the bridge for a while and looked into the water; it was grey and murky. In the pale yellow willow bushes off to one side lay several corpses, their bodies all intertwined – little black skeletons with shrivelled-up flesh; they had been burnt almost to a crisp. The weeds along the bank were already weaving in and out of their remains.

I decided to take the risk of going on a little farther in the direction of Fulda. The landscape became grey, then black. The valley seemed to have been swept clean. Only an occasional tree trunk stood upright; a few flattened cars in the street were a reminder that people had lived here at one time. The meadows were scorched, the fields seared to the ground, the woods burnt up, destroyed, without any foliage. Only along the banks of the river could you see traces of green.

When I got to a vantage point from which I should have been able to see Fulda, I turned back. I didn't bring anything home from this hike. Not even mushrooms could grow in the Fulda valley any more.

"And even so," my father said when I told him what I had seen, "it could only have been a small bomb. Fulda wasn't any metropolis. Whoever dropped the bomb was being economical. It didn't take much to wipe out that little place."

Once Father and I hiked off together towards the east to try to find bacon or fat of some kind for Mother. We came to the East German border. The watch-towers were empty, and weeds were sprouting on the ploughed strip along the fence. We could see into a valley where the fence had been knocked down and the posts broken off. It looked as if someone had driven through it with a bulldozer. In several places, some of them close to us, the wire fence had been cut, and trampled paths led through each of the openings.

A man with a stubbly beard came in our direction along the path nearest to us. He had a knapsack on his back and a child in one arm. He was gently pushing another child along in front of him. As we watched him, we held our breath. But there were no gunshots, no barking dogs, no alarms. When he came up to us he gave a friendly greeting.

"You were really lucky that time," my father said.

"What do you mean?" the man asked. "Nobody gets shot at here any more. Not since the bomb went off. The only thing is, you have to be careful to keep to the paths. There are still mines everywhere."

"You mean anyone who wants to can escape to the West now?" my father asked in disbelief.

"Escape?" the man asked. "What for? Nobody tries to escape now. It's the other way around, in fact. More and more people are coming over from your side to ours. Here in Thuringia we got off relatively lightly; Eisenach, Gotha, and Erfurt were destroyed, of course, and the cloud from Fulda took care of Meiningen and Suhl. But around here people can get by pretty well, assuming they survived typhoid fever and dysentery."

"But *you're* trying to escape, aren't you?" Father asked.

"Me?" The man looked surprised. "You mean because of the knapsack? Good God, no. That would be pretty stupid of me, seeing that things are supposed to be much worse on your side. I'm just going to visit relatives in that village right over there."

My father still seemed puzzled. "So there's no border here any more?"

"Not that I know of. Why should there still be borders when everything's been destroyed? All the major cities east of here were wiped out, and they say there wasn't a stone left standing in the whole Berlin area."

"So we're one country again?" my father asked.

"Looks that way," the man said. "But what do we know? All we hear are rumours. And public order's become a joke. Everybody has the same slogan now: Survive however you can, even if it's at somebody else's expense."

"That's right," my father said. "We've forgotten all our good upbringing. It's a case of only the strongest surviving."

"That's the way it is, all right," the man replied. He took off his knapsack, reached inside, and handed me a side of bacon.

"Here," he said. "You could use some fat. You look like the suffering Jesus himself. By the way, if you're going along the border you can make the fastest time on our side; the road that the patrols used to drive along is still there. I see lots of people riding by on bikes. Well, happy survival!"

He picked up the smaller child again and went on his way. We hardly had time to thank him.

"Why don't we go over to the East if they still have bacon there?" I asked.

"I don't know," Father said, "everything is so uncertain. There might just be someone who still feels it's his duty to patrol the border. After all, things can't have changed all that fast. What would become of Mother if they arrested me?"

I offered to go over alone. But he didn't want that either. "You can never tell. It's all just a lot of rumours."

We walked a short distance along the fence, each thinking his own thoughts, and then headed back. Along the way we asked for fat at a few more farmhouses, but no one gave us any.

"There's already been more than a dozen of you spongers here today," one farmer woman said. "This isn't any ginger-bread house."

And an old farmer snarled, "One-and-a-half men, eh? Forget it! If I give anything away, it's only to women with little children, or to pregnant ones. You two can get by on your own."

"My wife *is* pregnant," my father said. "And we have a small child at home."

"Anybody can say that," the man snapped at him.

So we did as he suggested and tried to get by on our own: when we had left the farmyard, we chased a chicken into a corner behind the barn. Father was able to catch hold of it, but he didn't have the heart to wring its neck right away. It beat its wings and cackled excitedly. The farmer must have heard it because he let the dog loose. It came racing up to us, barking furiously, and went for our legs. Father had to let the chicken go. He hit the dog across the back with a stake he picked up off a woodpile and it retreated with a yowl. I felt sorry for the poor thing. But I felt even more sorry that the chicken had got away.

"You know," Father said as we walked on, "the farmer really was in the right."

All the way back home he kept silent and seemed lost in thought. As dusk came, we dug up a few more potatoes in a secluded field and filled our knapsacks with them. If we hadn't been given the side of bacon, it would have been a wasted day for us. I resolved that the next time I went scrounging for food I would go alone. I was still a child; the farmers hardly ever sent me away without giving me something, even if it was nothing more than a beet.

We didn't get home until after midnight. Mother had already started to worry about us. She was very depressed; that afternoon, while she and Jens were hanging up strings of apple slices in Grandfather's workshop, someone had sneaked into our cellar and stolen half our supplies. Most of the potatoes that we had gathered during the last few weeks were gone. Carrots and heads of cabbage were missing, too. The thief had calmly put them in bags and passed them through the cellar window to an accomplice. It had to be someone from the neighbourhood. He must have seen Father and me leaving the house early that morning.

"We need a dog," Father said, fuming with rage.

"What would we feed him?" Mother asked.

From then on we never left Mother alone in the house. If Father went somewhere, I stayed with her, and if I went out foraging for food, Father stayed home. It took a long time for us to make up our losses this way. To make matters worse, it was getting more and more dangerous to steal from the fields. One day Father came home groaning; his shirt was torn and his nose was bleeding. A farmer had caught him stealing turnips and had beaten him brutally.

Even when there was nothing left in the fields, we kept going out every day to get wood. Sometimes Father went, sometimes I did. We would ride Grandfather's old bicycle. Once the tyres were beyond repair, we rode on the rims. We loaded the wood on an ancient two-wheeled trailer that had been in Grandfather's shed. Every day we tried to load it higher, lashing the wood down with rope. We competed against each other to see who could make the biggest load. Whoever stayed home that day chopped the wood into pieces that would fit into the stove.

We didn't need to fight over wood yet. Schornberg Forest was full of dry branches and fallen trees. And even charred wood gave off heat. But we didn't have many axes or saws. Someone stole our best saw one day when I went into the kitchen for a minute to have something to eat. Father was raging with anger.

"If I catch that guy, I'll kill him!" he roared.

I believed him.

During the day we spent most of our time in the kitchen now, because that was where the stove was. It was the only warm room in the house. At night we slept in the unheated rooms.

When all four of us were home, it got very cramped; the kitchen was only about ten-by-twelve feet. And Jens couldn't stay in one spot; he needed room to play. He complained a lot now, and Father got more and more impatient.

"He can't help it," Mother said.

"Yes, I know," Father sighed.

Everything took place in the kitchen: that was where we dried our shoes, which were almost worn out; Mother did the laundry there by hand, then strung a line from one wall to the other and hung it up to dry. The kitchen smelled of cooking odours and ash, soap suds, and sweat. But that didn't bother us. The kitchen was our home.

8

In September the first cases of radiation sickness began to show up among the townspeople. It took a different course than it had with the refugees from the Fulda area I'd seen in the hospital. Most of them had died after only a few days. But now the sickness dragged on and on. Only in the case of a few children was it over with more quickly; they died of leukaemia, most people assumed.

"It's starting now," Father said when he was alone with me. "The creeping death. Sooner or later we'll all have our turn; it's only a matter of what the sequence will be. And it goes nice and slowly, so that no one panics."

He was right. It never turned into a mass dying. People died slowly and alone, sometimes of diseases of the blood, sometimes of damage to internal organs – but the real cause was always the same: radiation.

October came, then November – it began to snow. Jens couldn't remember the last snowfall he'd seen. He was having a wonderful time trying to catch the snowflakes. We had a snowball fight. Mrs. Kramer looked out of the neighbour's house, completely bewildered. She hadn't heard laughter like ours for a long time. Or had she? During the typhoid epidemic, when there was no one left to look after the children at the castle, she had taken two of them under her wing. One of them soon died of dysentery, but the other one – a six-year-old girl with burn scars on her hands – was still alive. Ever since the child had been in her care, the people she was staying with had complained. But she wouldn't give her up.

Tears came to my mother's eyes as she watched us. She must have been thinking about Kerstin and Judith. Only a year ago Kerstin had greeted the first snowfall with the same enthusiasm.

We ran out of matches. Grandfather's lighter had long since been empty, and the flint was worn out anyway. From now on we had to keep the fire going overnight as well as during the day – at least enough to ignite a wood shaving from the embers the next morning. Almost every day someone knocked on the door: "Could you spare me some embers, Mrs. Bennewitz?"

Sometimes we were so tired that we didn't wake up when it was time to re-kindle the fire. Then the stove would be cold the next morning and I would have to go around the neighbourhood asking for embers. Fire had become the most important necessity to life, next to food.

If you could call what we ate food, that is. If anyone had put such miserable stuff in front of us in the old days, we would have refused to eat it. When we came back from holiday trips, Father often used to say to friends, "The hotel had a great location – right on the beach. But the food! It wasn't fit to eat!" And yet, all this meant was that the veal cutlets had been a little tough, or that the soup had too much garlic in it. Now, though, we would have devoured that hotel food ravenously and found it delicious – they could even have served us octopus with jam on it!

We had turnips and potatoes almost every day now, both for lunch and supper. And for breakfast we ate porridge made of grain that Mother had ground in Grandmother's coffee mill – cooked in water, and without milk or sugar. We had to use salt sparingly, too. It was already getting scarce in town and was valuable for bartering with. For a long time we had been using rock salt. The food didn't have much flavour, but we ate anything that was edible.

I'll never forget the first Christmas Eve after the bomb. In celebration of the event, Mother had opened the door to the living room. It was almost pitch-dark in there, because we had boarded up the windows for the winter and stuffed the cracks with hay and straw. It took a long time for that large a space to get warm enough for us to sit there without shivering. Mother splurged and got one of Grand-mother's candles out, a little red one that was left over from the last Christmas. She put it on the table in a wreath made out of pine twigs and lit it. We sat in a circle and gazed into the unaccustomed light. On other evenings all we could allow ourselves was the glow of the fire from the stove; by seven or eight o'clock we would go to bed. What a wonder-ful light it made, this candle flame! We watched it flickering and listened solemnly to the tinkling of the musical boxes which Mother had taken out of Grandmother's cabinet. She wound them up one after another, last of all the new one that we had brought along to give to Grandmother. Again it tinkled 'It's Now or Never'. Jens was awestruck. Later he played with his presents: the teddy bear from the hospital, which had been thoroughly washed, and the puppet that Mother had crocheted for him using old bits of wool. Father carved him a top. Jens was overjoyed.

But the rest of us couldn't help thinking about Kerstin and Judith and Silke and our grandparents. When Father noticed that Mother was crying, he took her hand and held it tightly. I laid my head in her lap the way I had when I was little and cried, too. But I kept my head under the table-top so that Jens wouldn't see me. Everyone wanted it to be a beautiful Christmas for him.

Once the candle had burned down, we had real roast

potatoes, browned in the last of the bacon that the man at the border had given us. After that, we each had a bowl of strawberries canned by Grandmother herself. The date was written on the canning jar: eleven days before the bomb.

The winter wasn't particularly cold. But it was hard enough on those who hadn't gathered enough firewood, and on the refugees who had no roof over their heads and still tottered along the streets. The homeless children had it worst of all; orphaned or separated from their parents, they looked miserable and neglected. Many didn't have shoes. Some had wrapped rags around their feet, others actually went barefoot and got frostbitten.

Whenever one of these children knocked at our door, Mother would heat up a bowl of turnip soup. If it was evening, the child was allowed to sleep in the kitchen in front of the stove. But the next morning there were often heart-rending scenes. The child wouldn't want to go, but would plead to stay just one more night where there was warmth and something to eat and a place to call home.

But Mother was firm.

"I can't take on more than I can cope with," she said. "When I let those poor little creatures stay with us for even a few days, I get attached. Then I can't bear to put them out of the house again."

Father agreed with her.

"People have to be hard-hearted if they want to survive in such hard times," he said at one point. "What good is Christian charity if it kills you?"

Some of the beggar-children had set themselves up in the cellar of the castle. The oldest ones were about fourteen, the youngest no more than two or three. Two teenaged girls were the leaders. Sometimes I walked past the castle and peered over at them out of the corner of my eye. Whenever anyone stopped and looked in their direction they automatically expected conflict.

"Get out of here," they shouted over to me, "or we'll beat the hell out of you!"

I'm sure they would have, too, if I hadn't left. They were a close-knit group. There were several cripples among them: an eight-year-old boy they called Willy was missing his left eye and his left arm; a red-haired kid named Robert dragged his right leg when he walked. On his back, he carried a schoolbag that he almost never put down. Grischa, who was five or six, had a face disfigured with scars.

I knew him and a few of the others from the time Mother and Judith had taken care of the children at the castle. One boy they called Andreas had no legs; they pushed him around in an old baby carriage. It was hard to tell his age, but judging by his face and his voice he was at least fourteen. Once when I was there he had a couple of the smaller children push him all the way around the castle. Every so often he had them stop so that he could write

Parents be DAMNED!

on the light-coloured walls. He printed the words with charcoal on all four sides. They were big enough to be seen from quite a distance.

There was a blind girl there, too, no older than eight or nine. She was always guided by a younger girl who had no face left. Her nose was nothing but a stump. You could see her teeth through a big hole in her cheek. Her other cheek and her forehead were furrowed with deep scars. Then there was a boy nicknamed Fuzzy who didn't seem to be quite normal. Every now and then he would start to scream horribly without any apparent reason and grab onto the person who happened to be nearest. Usually the girl with no face would come running then, put her arm around him, and stay with him until he calmed down again.

Apart from these, I remember three other small, frail children – I never found out for sure if they were boys or girls. All three had curly blonde hair. At first glance there didn't seem to be anything wrong with them. But after a while I found out that they were deaf. The oldest one, who I thought was probably a girl, stumbled when she walked. I told my mother about them.

"Their eardrums were probably pierced," she speculated. "And it sounds like the oldest one's inner ear was damaged. Poor things."

I liked to watch the two older girls best. They were both named Nicole. Their breasts were developing, but they had the faces of little children. One had coffee-coloured skin and dark eyes. I wondered if someone had adopted her and brought her here from a foreign country. She had a bright red scar diagonally across her forehead, which she tried to hide by combing her long, straight black hair over it. The other Nicole had freckles and very pale skin. A new growth of light blonde downy hair was sprouting on her head. She was missing a thumb.

I ran into the two Nicoles all over town. They were constantly out begging food for 'their' children and never seemed to get tired. They would spit at people who didn't give them anything and snarl, "I hope the radiation gets you, you rotten pig!" or something like that. Many people slipped them a boiled potato or a carrot purely out of fear.

What they didn't get for their children during the day-time, they stole at night. One time the dark-skinned Nicole bit Mrs. Lipinski on the hand; she had been caught late one evening in the Lipinskis' cellar just as she was about to make off with a carefully guarded sausage. Mr. and Mrs. Lipinski were known for their selfishness. They wouldn't share their embers with anyone, or give a beggar anything to eat, and they never helped to clear away rubble. People said that their cellar was still stacked high with food. Nicole got away with the sausage. A few minutes later Mr. Lipinski came rushing into the castle cellar in a rage, but the sausage was already gone – the children had eaten it up as fast as they could. The smallest ones were sitting in the laps of the two Nicoles, still chewing away. What could he do but turn around and go back? After all, he could hardly retrieve the sausage from their stomachs.

"If I catch you in town I'll kill you," he yelled at the girls. "I don't care if you *are* only children."

"Go ahead," the blonde Nicole replied. "But then it'll be your fault if all these kids starve to death – you bloody skinflints don't give a damn about them!"

"Bastards!" the boy with no legs shouted after him. "The bomb was your fault! You didn't care what happened to the children – the only thing you were interested in was having an easy life. Well, now you've got what you deserved. But you had to drag us along with you! I hope you rot in hell!"

Full of indignation, Mrs. Lipinski told everyone she met what the children had said.

The Nicoles and their gang were really becoming a public nuisance. But ever since the time I saw them dividing their booty among the little children and cuddling the smallest ones on their laps, I admired them in secret and was on their side. And I wasn't the only one in Schevenborn who defended them.

One morning someone found the dark-haired Nicole next to the Lipinskis' house with her head smashed in. Mr. Lipinski went around bragging that he had killed her.

"*She* won't be stealing any more sausages," he said. "Now we just have to get that other bloodsucker and everything will be peaceful again."

But the next night, half the town banded together in front of the Lipinskis' house, broke into their cellar, and cleaned it out. Mr. Lipinski had a stroke and remained paralysed afterwards. No one felt sorry for him. People felt that justice had been done.

I was one of the band who cleaned out the cellar. I carried off two sides of bacon and two sausages; one of the sausages was torn out of my hands a minute later. I took what I still had over to the castle rather than to my parents' house. The children had carried Nicole back and were huddled around her; she was frozen stiff. Her arms were raised as if she had been defending herself and her eyes stared wide open. I put the sausage and the bacon on the cellar steps and ran off.

I don't know where they buried her, or even *if* they buried her. How could they have dug a grave in the middle of winter without pickaxes and spades?

The other Nicole died towards the end of December, probably from exhaustion. Not long after that I found the three deaf children frozen to death in one corner of the castle cellar, right under another inscription; Andreas must have written it in several different parts of the castle. The remaining children kept roaming through the town for some time. A couple of them were lucky and found people to stay with. The others gradually disappeared – some froze to death, but most of them starved.

It was only a few days after the blonde Nicole had died that I saw Andreas's carriage sitting in the snow under a tree on the castle grounds. The snow was coming down hard and beginning to cover him and the carriage. I thought at first that Andreas must have frozen to death, but he was alive. He had torn his blanket into strips with his swollen red hands and braided them into a thick rope. When he saw me coming, he hid it quickly and stared at me spitefully. He had an intelligent face. I noticed how long his eyelashes were.

"You can't just sit here in the cold," I said.

"Don't worry, I'm leaving," he said sullenly. "It's just taking me a while, because my hands are so stiff."

"Do you want me to push you somewhere?" I asked. "Anywhere you want, except – I can't take you home with me. My parents wouldn't allow it."

"No," he answered, "I wouldn't want to go to your house anyway, even if you wanted to have me. Not any more. If you want to help me, let's get started. Just don't ask any dumb questions. Take this rope and throw it over that branch there."

He pulled out the rope and handed it to me. It was pretty long. It must have taken him a long time to tear up the blanket and braid the pieces together. I threw it over the branch and put the two ends in Andreas's hands. He sat up straighter and made a big loop. I was trying to work out what he was up to. It finally became clear to me when he put his head through the loop.

"Are you crazy?" I shouted, and pulled it off his head.

Then he started to plead with me. I stood next to the carriage, put my cold hands in my pants pockets, and tried not to look at Andreas. It was snowing down the back of my collar.

"On the day the bomb went off I lost my legs," he said. "Everyone else in my family was killed instantly. I had the bad luck of not bleeding to death. Nicole – the one with the blonde hair – knew me from before. She lived two houses down from me. She bandaged me up as well as she could and then she put me in her dead sister's carriage and pushed me here. With her gone, there's no one to take care of me. I'm lost without her."

"Yes," I said. "I see what you mean."

"Am I supposed to wait till I starve?" he demanded. "For three days I haven't eaten anything except snow. Please help me. I'll take full responsibility. All you have to do is pull the carriage out from under me."

I thought about it for a while. I chewed on my lower lip and wondered if I should just run away. But that would have been the most cowardly way of avoiding the decision. So I tried to string it out.

"Do you think people see each other again when they're dead?" I asked. "Like their parents?"

"My parents?" he replied morosely. "I don't want to see them again. They can go to hell, and everybody else's parents, too. They could have prevented all this. They saw

84

it coming and they didn't even *try* to protect us from this destruction. Why did they even have us, if they didn't care about us any more than that?"

The noose swung back and forth between us. Snowflakes were gathering on it.

"I go in my pants and I have to sit in it," he said. "I'm nothing but sores. Nicole kept me clean and brought me food. She's gone now. Can't you understand that I want to get out of this misery? I'm not really living any more. Please!"

He took the noose in his hand again. This time I didn't tear it away from him. He looked at me for a second, then put it around his neck.

"I'm ready," he said. "Be sure you pull really hard, okay?"

I swallowed hard and grabbed the handle. I pulled the carriage with all my might and ran with it for a few steps, then let go of it and kept running. I didn't look back until I had reached the edge of the castle grounds. Andreas was still swinging back and forth.

A few hours later I went back and cut him down. He was covered with snow. No one had taken the carriage; it had tipped over and was lying under the new snow. All you could see was a little mound. I put Andreas in the carriage. He wasn't at all heavy, thin as he was and without any legs. I pushed him over to the woods on the other side of town. On the way I met Mrs. Kernmeyer, who was carrying a big load of wood. She asked me what I had in the carriage. I told her it was rubbish. Luckily she didn't look under the canopy. I'm sure she would have asked me why I was going to so much trouble for some dead boy I hardly even knew.

I pushed Andreas to the old abandoned quarry where I used to play during the holidays. I had discovered a small cave there once. It was so hidden away that no one else seemed to have ever found it. The entrance was behind a hollow tree; you had to crawl between the roots to get in. There was so little space inside that you could only crouch and barely had room to stretch out your arms. I didn't need this cave any more now; I couldn't imagine that I would ever play there again. So I scraped away the snow around the entrance and pushed Andreas inside. The cave was just big enough to hold him. I shoved a big flat stone in front of the opening. It took a lot of effort to pry it loose from the ground. It was a cold day.

At first I was going to dump the carriage over the edge into the quarry, but then I thought about the new brother or sister who was coming and decided to push it home. I flung the dirty mattress down into the quarry. The new baby couldn't lie on that – not on that!

When I got home I told my parents that I had found the carriage by the castle, which wasn't a lie. Mother was thrilled. She lost no time in cleaning it up and fitting it out. For days she bugged Father and me by showing us every little step in her sewing projects. First she made a mattress using a partially burnt quilt that had been in the attic among Grandmother's stuff. Next came a little down blanket made from one of Grandmother's pillows and covered with white damask that still bore her monogram.

"Isn't this sweet?" she asked again and again, looking for praise. Father and I cast glances at each other, but of course we acted enthusiastic. It did make us happy that she had livened up again and wasn't thinking constantly about the dead and the past.

9

In January the third wave of death began in Schevenborn. This time the townspeople didn't die during an epidemic, but from starvation. Few of the dogs that were still in the town survived that winter. No one felt disgusted any more at the thought of eating dog meat.

Some people went mad, though, like Dreesen, the young man who had helped out at the hospital. He had washed and polished his red sports car all summer and autumn. It hadn't got burned-out or crushed by debris, and the garage at his parents' house was still standing. When anyone asked Dreesen, "Why are you doing that? You can't drive anywhere now," he would just laugh. Since the explosion he had been carting rubble off the streets in a wheelbarrow; he worked in Fulda Road, the Back Road, Wall Lane and in our neighbourhood by the South Gate. People had told him what a good job he was doing, and many of them had helped him. Since Christmas we had been able to make our way up Wall Lane to the Back Road, turn off from there onto Fulda Road, then walk along the curve and back down to the South Gate – all without having to climb over piles of rubble. We owed this to Dreesen.

But now, in January, the townspeople were presented

with a strange sight: one bright Sunday, when there was almost no snow left on the ground, Dreesen backed his glistening car out of the garage, turned up his cassette player as loud as it would go, and drove for hours around and around the four streets he had cleared. His parents tried to stop him and calm him down, but he nearly ran them over. He didn't seem to hear a thing. He drove and drove, so fast that he barely made it around the corners. The music from his stereo blasted through the whole town. Everyone except those who were dying felt drawn to his racing strip. A car! Music! It was like the old days before the bomb. Several people started to cry. And Jens gazed in wonder. He didn't remember what a moving car looked like. For him, this red sports car was something miraculous.

The music got to my mother. She had always loved music, but only classical. Schubert was her favourite composer. She couldn't stand what she called 'that pop howling'. But now the songs Dreesen was playing, which grew louder or softer depending on where his car was at the time, brought tears to her eyes. All the old, familiar, trite melodies: *Ghengis Khan; Don't Cry for Me, Argentina; A Little Bit of Peace* and lots of others, all played over and over again. None of us wanted to miss a song, even though our hands and feet had gone numb with cold.

When his tank was almost empty, Dreesen went racing straight down the street instead of taking the turn from Fulda Road towards the South Gate. With his foot on the pedal he rammed into a pile of rubble that was more than a storey high and filled the whole width of the street. The pile is still there now and probably always will be. A jet of flame shot out of Dreesen's beautiful car. He burned to death in it. That must have been what he wanted. The music continued to come out of the burning wreck for a few seconds, and then died with a strange sigh.

The townspeople surrounded the car and warmed themselves by the flames, and then carried some of the embers home with them. For several days the only topic of conversation – when people said anything at all – was the car and the music.

"It was a beautiful death," my father said. "A classic death for a car-lover."

My mother's thoughts were getting muddled, too. Suddenly she wanted to get away from Schevenborn. She brought it up time and time again.

"But where would we go?" Father asked. "Especially now, in the middle of winter."

"Where do you think?" Mother cried angrily. "To Bonames, of course!"

"You're mad!" Father said, annoyed. "Bonames is part of Frankfurt, and Frankfurt isn't there any more. Can't you understand that, Inge?"

"Bonames is quite a way out," Mother replied. "And our street doesn't face the centre of the city. We own a condominium, Klaus. It's ours – we can't just give it up! Irene Kellermann is a reliable woman. I'm sure she's kept her eye on it like a watchdog!"

"But Inge –" Father sighed.

"We have a cellar full of provisions there, and all our winter clothing; power and water must have been restored long ago –"

"Inge!" Father shouted and shook her. "Come to your senses! You're living in a dream world. Do you want to give birth to a child in a pile of ashes?"

"Am I supposed to have it here, where we'll either suffocate inside or freeze to death outside? Where we're starving? Where all we see are ruins when we look out the door? It smells like animal carcasses and burnt human flesh here! Is this the kind of world we want to offer our baby?"

"The kind of world we could offer a child in good conscience probably doesn't exist any more in all of Europe," Father said. "Here, at least, we know what we've got: a roof over our heads, a wardrobe full of your parents' clothing, a stove and wood for keeping us warm. Can't you see that

89

we're incredibly well-off in comparison to most people? If you're able to breast-feed the baby during the first few months, it'll have a good chance of making it."

"How am I supposed to do that? Look how thin I am!" she yelled. "Even Kerstin had to be started on a bottle after three weeks."

"Back then you didn't really want to breast-feed because of your figure. But now it's a matter of survival. You'll *have* to! You've got to start eating more. And you've got to look at things more positively."

"The Kernmeyers still have powdered milk," I said. "Maybe they'd give us some for a saw or an axe –"

"How is powdered milk going to help me?" Mother asked in despair. "*Hope* is what I need. Without hope the baby won't even be born alive. In Bonames there's bound to be some semblance of order by now. They simply *have* to restore order to a part of the country as densely populated as the Rhine–Main area. There must be capable people there who can do what might otherwise seem impossible. And even if each person only gets half a pint of milk a day and a pound of bread a week – at least we'd know we could count on it, just like after World War II. God knows our parents told us about that often enough, so often that I got sick of hearing it. Even if it's only tiny amounts of food – we'd have a right to it. Think what that would mean! Here everyone's constantly looking for an opportunity to take something away from somebody else. We have to be on guard around the clock!"

"It's not just here," Father said wearily. "It's got to be that way wherever there are any survivors."

"But I can't stand this!" Mother cried. "It's driving me crazy! And think how it must be affecting the baby, Klaus. Let's go back to Bonames, please – before this place kills us –"

For days she pleaded, and for days Father tried to come up with new arguments to convince her. But she wasn't really listening to him.

"No one knows for sure if Frankfurt was destroyed," she said. "We haven't heard any official announcements. It's all rumours. In horrible times like these, rumours make every disaster seem even worse. My parents found that out during the last war."

"To make this disaster any worse than it is," Father answered, "is beyond the scope of the human mind."

"What do you know?" she snapped. "Human beings are capable of anything!"

"That's right," he sighed.

"So you admit that Frankfurt still might be there?"

"No," he said. "Not Frankfurt, and not Bonames, either."

"Prove it to me!" she shouted in a rage. "I won't give up until you do."

He couldn't, of course. She wasn't even convinced when Father brought a man home with him who was from Praunheim, another suburb of Frankfurt; he had come to Schevenborn to see if his relatives had any grease and potatoes. He and his wife had been on holiday in the Oden Forest and had walked back to Frankfurt after the explosion. His wife had died of typhoid fever in the meantime. He reported that Frankfurt was completely destroyed – it had simply disappeared. Praunheim, too. The whole Rhine–Main area as far down as Darmstadt and over to Mainz was a desert of ash.

Mother didn't say much the whole time he was there. Father gave him a few potatoes, and the man couldn't thank him enough. When he left I noticed that he was limping; he had bags tied around his feet and ankles. He looked like an old man, although he had mentioned that he was thirty-six.

As soon as he had left, Father said to Mother, "Now you've heard it from an eye-witness."

"The hell I have!" she stormed. "How do we know if he was telling the truth? Do you know this man? Are you sure he's from Praunheim? He told you what you wanted to hear. He was just after the potatoes!"

In the wake of starvation, a flu epidemic broke out. From what we heard it had spread through the whole area. If everyone had been healthy and had enough to eat it wouldn't have been that serious, but for the half-starving it spelled doom. Once again there were dead bodies that had to be burned; the ground was frozen and it would have taken several pits to contain them all. The whole town stank again of burnt hair and flesh.

When Mother found out about the flu epidemic, which we had kept secret from her for a long time, she started to panic.

"Not *another* one of us!" she wailed. "Not Roland, not Jens! Oh God, not the baby –"

She was half-crazed with fear; she wouldn't drink any water, touch a door handle, or eat. All she wanted was to leave, to get away from Schevenborn, away from the flu, away from danger.

"Inge," Father said in desperation, "it would mean the end for all of us if we left here!"

"You're confused," she said with tears in her eyes. "You're not able to think clearly any more. I'll save us. You'll all be saved if you come with me!"

Father threw himself onto the sofa and buried his face in his hands.

10

When I went into the kitchen the next morning, my mother had Grandmother's winter coat on and was rummaging around in the pram. She was wearing her old hiking boots, and one of our suitcases lay open on the kitchen table. The other one was already packed and stood by the door. Jens was all bundled up and hopping around with excitement and expectation. The fire in the stove was out.

"Dad!" I called anxiously. "Come quick –"

Father came rushing into the kitchen with puffy eyes.

"No!" he shouted. "We're staying here!"

"*You* can stay if you want," Mother said calmly.

"The children are staying, too!"

"Then I'll go alone," she said with a mocking smile. "Just the baby and me. You can't stop me."

She was right, we couldn't stop her. And so, two hours later, we all left together. I was going to put on my leather pants that I had been wearing the day of the explosion. They didn't fit any more, though; they were much too short. Father's trousers were still too big for me, so I put on Grandfather's. I had to wear braces with them because they were so wide.

Father had put the two suitcases along with our sleeping-bags into the bicycle trailer and had tied a bulging overnight bag onto the basket. He and I carried knapsacks full of potatoes, apples, mushrooms, carrots, and turnips. I pushed the bicycle and he pushed the carriage. Jens, who was sitting in the pram, soon started to complain because another small suitcase was lying across his legs. It was filled with baby clothes that Mother had sewed, knitted, or crocheted during the winter, using Grandmother's supplies of material and yarn. The only thing Mother carried was a shoulder bag containing family documents and the money that we had left.

"Why are you taking the money?" Father asked.

"I'm sure we'll be able to use it again in Bonames," she replied.

He let her have her way and merely shook his head.

Mrs. Kramer was standing at our door with her foster child when we left. She had agreed to move into our grandparents' house and keep an eye on it.

"Only while we're away," Father had emphasised, "so that no refugees try to move in or take things."

Through the whole winter Mrs. Kramer had had to make do with one room at the Mackenhausers'. She had constantly quarrelled with them, mostly because of the child. So it wasn't surprising that she was overjoyed to be able to move into our house. Now she would have a stove and wood and the few potatoes and carrots that were left over in the cellar. She pretended, of course, that she was heart-broken to see us leave, but she could hardly conceal her pleasure. I didn't trust her.

"Why didn't you let *me* stay and take care of the house?" I asked Father. We were finally on our way up the road to Lanthen, out of breath after the effort of clambering over the piles of rubble at the edge of town.

"I considered that," he answered. "But it would have been hard for us with all the luggage. And it's better if we stick together, no matter what happens. We're all we have left."

In spite of the luggage, he and I could move faster than Mother. She was getting pretty big. The baby was only two months away now; it was due around the end of March or the beginning of April. She panted as she came up the hill behind us.

"This is madness, madness," Father moaned, so softly that Mother couldn't hear him.

"When do you think we'll be back?" I asked him. I kept my voice down, too.

"I'm hoping that she'll decide to turn around soon. She simply can't take this. Maybe a week, maybe even today."

But he was deceiving himself. She kept on going and never complained. Lost in thought and with her head bent low, she strode onwards. Sometimes, when Jens couldn't stand being in the pram any longer, she took him by the hand and let him walk alongside her. He was her friend. She told him about our apartment in Bonames, and then they talked about the new baby; she said it would be called either Jessica Marta or Boris Alfred. The second names had been Grandmother's and Grandfather's.

We came to the place where we had left our car on the day of the explosion. The pine tree was still lying across the road, and our car stood next to it, covered with snow. It even still had its tyres. But then, who would have gone to the effort of taking them off? I tried the doors – they were frozen shut.

I pressed my nose against the rear window and breathed on the frost. As it melted, I could see inside. I could make out two children, crouching on the back seat with their legs pulled up. They were little girls, one with her head resting on the shoulder of the other one. I knew them. It was the blind girl from the castle cellar and the girl with the mutilated face – the two who had always been together. Their eyes were closed.

"There are two kids sleeping inside," I whispered to Father. He gave a surprised look and peered in through the hole in the ice. Then he looked at me in distress. "They're

95

not sleeping – they're dead. Frozen stiff."

"Don't you think we could drive for a while?" Mother asked when she had caught up with us. "We could at least get as far as the next tree on the other side of Wietig –"

"What's the point?" Father said.

"All right," she sighed, "let's just keep walking."

Jens ran up to the car and wanted to look in. But we quickly put him into the pram and moved on.

Beyond Wietig, Mother slipped twice on the icy road that led through the forest. She was lucky, though, and fell both times into snow drifts at the side of the road. We spent the night on the other side of Lanthen in a shelter by a pasture.

Our luck seemed to be holding out the next day, too; it started to thaw. The warmer weather lasted for a few days. During the whole first half of February the temperature stayed above freezing point.

We had become too tough by then to let any kind of weather bother us, even though we sometimes slept in damp sleeping-bags in barns and plodded our way through snow and mud in shoes that were no longer watertight. Just six months earlier we would never have got rid of sniffles and cold sores, coughs and sore throats after a hike like that – assuming we didn't come down with pneumonia. But now, not even Jens got sick.

The only problem we had was with the pram. We spent a whole day looking for a wheel to replace one that had broken. We finally found one in a rubbish dump where crowds of people from nearby villages were burrowing around.

We were making slow progress. Mother, who had once been such an active hiker, couldn't walk very fast any more because the baby was getting so heavy. Still, she never said what we were hoping she would: "I can't go any farther. Let's turn back."

The route that Father had chosen went over Bird Mountain. He had hoped to find roads there that were reasonably passable, places to stay for the night, even an occasional hospitable farm with a glass of milk or a bowl of nourishing soup. But it soon became apparent to us that we weren't going to find many people who were willing to help. Now that we had left Schevenborn, we belonged to the outsiders, the refugees, the beggars, who plodded their way through the country. Whenever we approached a house, the door would close, a dog would begin to bark, or we would notice a crudely painted sign:

BEGGING POINTLESS HAVE NOTHING OURSELVES!

A few villages were fenced in with barbed wire. Guards stood at the gates.

"Keep away!" they would call out from a good distance. "Nobody gets in here. Your kind have brought us typhoid fever and dysentery; a third of our villagers have died. We don't want any more epidemics. We'll kill anyone who tries to get in by force. We've had enough."

"I suppose they're right," Father said. "Our problem is, now *we're* the ones who have to stand outside the fence."

If we hadn't been living in such misery, it would have been a beautiful hike, especially because there weren't any cars. Only once in a while did a cart drawn by horses or cows come past, or a bicycle. But no one gave a friendly greeting. And all the hardship was depressing: starving people from the devastated valleys were coming to the mountains to try to find food; the homeless begged for a room or even a place in a hayloft; children asked us if we had seen their parents; the sick and the dying lay along the roadside next to dead bodies. We saw people who were wasted to the bone; there were cripples, people who had gone insane or been blinded, mutes and bald-headed people and, time after time, people with horrible burn scars. They walked in our direction, our paths crossed, they caught up with us, or we caught up with them. We asked them what they knew, and they asked us what we knew. It would have been easy to think that everyone who was still alive was on the road, wandering aimlessly through all of Germany. We met Czechs and Belgians, too, and people from Holland and France.

Some people claimed that the war was still going on. But nowhere did we come upon soldiers or battle lines. Others said that the war had been over for a long time, and still others, that there had never been one. The whole thing had just been a misunderstanding.

But my father refused to believe that.

We met people who were lugging the most ridiculous things along with them, like the old woman with the alabaster statue in her knapsack and the young man with the surfboard. Oil paintings, television sets, and cash registers were dragged for miles. Some items were used to barter with, others were kept for their sentimental value; still others were considered to be necessary for existence. One man we met had a jacket covered with military decorations, although he didn't have a shirt on underneath and could hardly walk upright because he was so hungry.

Most of the people were coming in our direction, from the Wetterau and Spessart regions, from Alsfeld and Marburg, even from as far away as Aschaffenburg. They all told of starvation and epidemics and the terrible radiation sickness in the areas around Frankfurt and the Kinzig Valley, which had received fall-out from the Frankfurt cloud. Hardly anyone had survived there.

"What about Frankfurt itself?" my mother asked.

"Doesn't exist any more. Wiesbaden's gone, too. So are Russelsheim, Hoechst, Hanau, and Offenbach. Nothing but mountains of rubble and ash as far as you can see."

"Did you see it with your own eyes?" Mother asked.

"With my own eyes? I'm not crazy. The whole region is contaminated. No one goes there voluntarily. But everyone knows that the Rhine–Main area is dead. There's not even a cockroach left."

"Do you see what I mean?" Mother said later to Father. "Everyone claims they know what happened, but no one knows for sure."

They had conversations like this two or three times a day. And she never failed to ask people we met where they were from.

A man from Friedberg, annoyed by her persistence, finally said to her, "If you want to meet somebody from Frankfurt, it'll have to be a corpse. There's hardly anything left of Friedberg, even – and we're almost thirty kilometres out."

When she heard that, Mother grew silent and walked on very slowly. But by the next morning she had either forgotten or repressed everything she hadn't wanted to hear and was striding out as fast as she could towards Frankfurt–Bonames.

"The best indication is that we haven't met anyone from Bonames yet," she said. "If Bonames had been destroyed, we would have come across someone from there by now."

"Think about Fulda," Father said, exhausted. "Did one single person from Fulda who'd been there on the day of the explosion show up in Schevenborn?"

She had no response to that.

In spite of everything, it was a good idea that Father had decided on the route over Bird Mountain. The dogs hadn't all been eaten here yet, and there were villages in which hardly a window-pane had been broken. There was no rubble lying around, the streets weren't blocked by fallen trees, and some of the isolated villages had even been spared the epidemics of typhoid fever. Once in a while we came across farmers who hadn't been hardened yet by all the misery passing by.

It took eighteen days to get as far as the Wetterau region.

We could have made it in less time, but Father insisted that Mother stop frequently to rest, that she go to bed early, and sleep as late as she could in the morning.

"We have to see that she doesn't get too weak," he said to me. "When we get to Frankfurt, she'll need all the strength she can muster, and then she'll have to walk the whole way back again."

We spent three nights in cattle shelters, another eight in barns; once a doctor's widow even let us use a heated room. Five times we spent the night in quarters set up for the homeless, and one other time in a picnic shelter in the woods. We had used our provisions sparingly. Our knapsacks weren't bulging any more, but they weren't empty either. Now and then a farmer offered us soup. A woman in a small remote village gave us a loaf of home-made bread. Even though it wasn't much bigger than a couple of rolls, we enjoyed it, taking tiny bites and chewing them slowly and thoughtfully. The taste of this bread reminded us so much of times past!

Near Schotten we walked past a field of winter rye. It had been planted in the autumn, long after the bomb. At first we couldn't believe our eyes. These tiny green seedlings under the thawing snow – a whole field of green shoots – seemed like a mirage to us.

"Just look at that!" my father exclaimed. "In a totally abnormal time like this, someone has done something absolutely normal. It's hard to believe."

We stood looking at the field for a long time. Then Mother said, "This is the kind of thing that gives a person hope."

Later on, in the Wetterau region, our good luck deserted us. The farther we went, the more devastated the villages were. There were hardly any people left. All along the streets lay half-decomposed bodies and animal carcasses. When we got to the ruins of Friedberg, it started to snow heavily. The streets disappeared from sight and there were no snowploughs; we got our bearings from the occasional signposts and street signs that hadn't been knocked down by the shock wave.

"Bonames?" a woman asked in surprise as she walked unsteadily past us. "Save yourselves the effort. There's nothing left there."

"Do you still want to go on?" Father asked Mother, who was bundled up to her nose and leaning against the wind.

"Yes," she said. "I have to see it with my own eyes."

We followed Father onto the Kassel–Frankfurt autobahn – or what was left of it. In many places the pavement was uneven and torn up, as if it had burst. The closer we got to Frankfurt, the bumpier it got; it looked as if it had melted. This was still the best place to walk, though, because the concrete slabs beneath the surface of the road lay exposed for long stretches at a time, allowing us firm footing and helping us to find our way in the blowing snow.

Snuggled together, we spent the night in a half-crushed public bathroom that stood under the remains of fallen trees on what had once been a car park. Jens and Mother slept deeply and breathed peacefully, but Father moaned in his sleep; he was awake long before it was light outside. I didn't sleep much that night, either; the bicycle was broken beyond repair and I was worried about how we would manage our luggage. My thoughts and dreams centred on Bonames. I would have liked to believe what Mother believed, but I knew that Father would turn out to be right.

The next morning we crawled stiffly into the light of day and saw a blinding white snowscape before us, stretching out in all directions under the clear blue sky and unmarred by any tracks. The sun was just rising. The snow was deep and we had to plough our way through. Mother was in a happy mood and joked with Jens and me. But Father pushed the pram on in silence; he didn't seem to want to talk to anyone.

We didn't meet a soul as we headed south. Alone on the road, we eventually came to the Bad Homburg exit. Mother plodded on impatiently. Father pushed the pram behind her and kept silent. It took a lot of effort to keep up with them; pulling or pushing the bicycle trailer without the bicycle was difficult. It had so much stuff in it.

"We should be able to see Bonames soon now," Mother called, looking off to the south. Before us lay a monotonous, gently rolling desert of snow in which not a single tree stood. Off in the distance a dark ribbon shimmered: the Main River.

There weren't any guard rails or signs here to guide us, but Father knew his way around the area. We had lived in Bad Homburg for years, and he had driven into Frankfurt every day on the autobahn. He looked for kilometre markers and examined bumps in the snow every now and then. Finally he found the exit to Bonames and we turned in that direction. Bonames was right next to the autobahn and we had always been able to see the high-rise buildings from some distance away. We left the road and made our way across a field.

"It's pretty hazy today," Mother said.

I didn't see any haze. You could see as far as the Taunus Mountains and Bird Mountain, and even to the foothills of the Oden Forest. When the ground began getting more uneven in front of us, Father stopped and cleared away the snow with his foot. What he uncovered was rubble.

"We're in Bonames," he announced.

I'll never forget Mother's eyes. She raised her hand and let it fall again. After a while she said, "Let's go back."

11

The trek back home was torture. Mother walked very slowly now. It seemed to us that she didn't *want* to walk any faster. Time and again she would stop, hold her stomach, and murmur, "The baby's kicking so much."

In the meantime the flu had broken out in the villages on Bird Mountain. Everywhere we went there was activity in the cemeteries. Many of the villages had been encircled with barbed wire. No one offered us soup any more, or a warm stable to spend the night in, although in March the weather had turned bitterly cold.

My knapsack was just about empty. During the last few days, all we'd had to eat were dried apple slices and mushrooms. The potatoes and carrots had run out some time ago, and there was only one withered turnip left. We licked snow when we were thirsty – and that was constantly. Our lips were parched and cracked.

Father killed a hungry terrier that had run up to us and snapped at our legs. He wanted to roast it, but there was no place to get fire. For days I carried the creature, frozen stiff, in my knapsack. When we were finally able to make a fire and thaw the dog, my father got sick to his stomach while he was butchering it. He had never done anything like that before. And Jens and I threw up all that we ate; our stomachs couldn't handle such an unaccustomed meal. For days we kept ourselves alive on the tough, half-raw remains of the dog meat, which disgusted me. Mother was the only one it didn't seem to bother, but then she didn't eat much, either. With her mind somewhere else, she would chew and chew until even the toughest piece was soft.

Once again we went past the field that had been planted in winter rye. At first we thought it was a different field, because we couldn't believe what we saw. But I distinctly remembered the three birches that stood along one edge. It *was* the same field! Tiny seedlings were visible between the snowdrifts.

They had turned yellow, and here and there even brown. "There won't be any harvest here this year," Father muttered sadly.

We slept every night now in open sheds next to pastures. Sometimes other refugees had beaten us to it and Father would have to fight for a place for us. We picked up lice and fleas, and two of Father's toes got frozen. To make matters worse, the bicycle trailer fell apart. There was no way it could be repaired.

On the other side of the village of Herbstein, Mother started to get feverish. It wasn't long before Jens had a temperature, too. The flu had caught up with us. We stayed for over a week in a field barn where there was still a pile of hay left over from the past year. It was big enough for all of us to burrow into and keep warm. We watched helplessly as Jens burned with fever and became rapidly weaker and more apathetic. Father ran to the nearest village to try to get some hot tea. But they wouldn't let him in – especially not when they found out he had been around sick people.

During the fourth night, I was awakened by Mother's loud, difficult breathing. Now and then she murmured a few words. I couldn't understand most of what she said.

I held her hand; it was burning hot. I was so afraid that I couldn't utter a sound. I groped around in the dark for Jens, who was lying next to Mother; I found his face and stroked it gently. He was ice-cold and didn't react to my touch. I heard the hay rustling and could tell that Father was lying there awake.

"Father," I whispered, relieved, "Jens isn't hot any more. His fever is gone."

"Yes," Father said with his voice breaking, "his fever is gone. He's dead."

The next morning we laid him under an elderberry bush behind the barn. It was freezing cold and in a few minutes he was stiff. I sneaked off a few times that day to look at him. It seemed to me now that I had been even fonder of him than Kerstin. She had been gone for so long; she was so far away. It didn't matter that Jens wasn't my real brother – I had forgotten that completely.

We didn't see how we could possibly bury him since the ground was frozen solid. Finally we decided to gather up stones. First we had to pound them loose from the earth. I thought again about how I had buried Andreas; that seemed a lifetime ago, although it was only a few weeks.

Burying the dead, constantly burying the dead – that was one of the chief occupations of the survivors. On that morning I wished I wasn't one of them. I envied Jens the peace he had found.

Slowly, very slowly, the pile of stones grew over him. If there were any crows left on Bird Mountain, they wouldn't get him, our dear little boy.

Mother survived the flu. Father told her as gently as he could that Jens had died. But she just nodded and didn't even cry. Father gave me a desperate look. A little later he said to me, "Maybe it's better that she's this way."

As we walked on in the direction of Schevenborn, we hardly said a word, but just brooded to ourselves. None of us could think clearly any more. We were exhausted.

Father led the way. The two suitcases and the sleeping-bags that had been in the bicycle trailer were stacked on top of the baby carriage now. Mother dragged behind. She didn't want anyone to help her. I followed along last, carrying my knapsack and the overnight bag.

And so we plodded on until almost the end of March – only a few miserable kilometres each day. When we found a half-decent place to stay, we sometimes didn't even get up the next morning.

A short distance before Lanthen, Mother collapsed. Father threw the two big suitcases down off the pram into the snow and told me to carry the small one with the baby clothes. Then he put Mother in her sleeping-bag and laid her across the other bags in the pram. We had to leave the suitcases behind.

Near Wietig, Mother went into labour. As soon as she told Father he started to move as fast as he could. We took turns pushing her. We ran right into a snowstorm. Snow swirled into the pram and Mother was shaking with cold. Father wrapped Jens's blanket around her legs which were hanging out between the bars of the handle; then he put my empty knapsack over her head to protect it from the snow, and covered her body with the baby blanket.

"No," she moaned, "not that blanket. It'll get damp, and what will we cover the baby with then?"

So Father took off Grandfather's thick turtleneck that he had been wearing under his hiking jacket and spread it over her. He must have been terribly cold now himself.

He tried to find a place to stay in Wietig. He beat on the doors and the plugged-up windows with his fists.

"There's a pregnant woman here!" he shouted. "She's already in labour! Don't people care about their fellow human beings any more?"

Nothing stirred. Father was crying with rage. We had to go on. Luckily it was downhill all the way after we got to Wietig Forest. He told me to run on ahead.

"Tell Mrs. Kramer to boil some water," he called after me, "and have her put a mattress in the kitchen and make sure it's warm there! Leave the suitcase in the house and come back as fast as you can. You'll have to help me get the pram over the rubble!"

I raced off. I hadn't run for a long time. My damp clothes, which I had been wearing for weeks, rubbed painfully against my body, and the suitcase bumped against my leg with every step. When I got to Schevenborn it was already evening. The town, or what was left of it, seemed lifeless. Through cracks here and there I saw the glimmer of dull light from stove fires. As I clambered over the mountains of rubble and ran on, I noticed that the hospital was gone; only a few charred bits of wall remained. The roof of the Kernmeyers' house, which stood on our corner, was burnt out. I rushed down the street towards my grandparents' house and saw with enormous relief that it was still standing and hadn't suffered any further damage. I pounded on the door with my fists.

I heard shuffling footsteps; the door opened a crack and Mrs. Kramer's distrustful face peered out.

"Go away," she said. "We don't have anything to spare."

"But it's *me*," I cried, "Roland! Don't you recognise me? We've come back!"

"What – you?" she said, aghast. I noticed how horrified she was. "I thought you'd all be –"

She didn't finish her sentence.

"Who's there?" I heard a man's voice growl from inside the house.

"You'd never guess, Karl! The Bennewitzes are back again!" she called. She kept her hand on the door handle. She didn't even let me into the hall. A hunched-over man came shuffling out of the kitchen. I didn't know him. He was wearing Grandfather's checked waistcoat.

"So what do you want?" he said when he saw me. "You people left, and that's that. You thought you'd be better off somewhere else."

I looked at Mrs. Kramer, who was standing behind him. "But my father worked that out with you! He said we'd be back soon. You were only supposed to –"

"I don't know anything about that," Mrs. Kramer said, pushing away the inquisitive-looking little girl who was standing behind her. "I can't remember any agreement like that. He just handed the house over to me and said that I could live in it from then on."

"That's not true!" I shouted. "I was there myself! And anyway, it's Grandfather's house. He's dead. So now it belongs to us!"

"Oh, my God!" the old man sneered. "Just listen to this kid! What's all this legal business? Don't you realise those times are past? People take what they need and they defend it. We'd sooner set this house on fire than give it back – you can tell your parents that. It would do us in. Shut the door, Marie, the snow's coming in."

I shoved my foot between the door and the jamb.

"But my mother is going to have a baby!" I yelled.

"Take your foot away!" Mrs. Kramer shrieked.

I pulled my foot out. The door slammed shut.

I knocked on a few more doors in the neighbourhood. Most of the time no one answered. Other people shut the door before I could even say my name. Only one old woman mumbled through the crack in the doorway, "There's already twelve of us here in one room. But if you need some embers, you can have 'em." I'd never seen her before. She must have been one of the refugees from the Fulda area.

I stood in the dusk with the suitcase and bag and cried in desperation. Then I suddenly thought of the castle. I ran over to the grounds. There it stood between the tall trees – stark and massive, grey and lonely. Setting the bags down by the outside staircase, I ran through the rooms. The floors were still crusted with filth from the past summer, and it had snowed through the large open window. The wind was howling through the empty rooms and the broad stairwell with its costly inlaid wood. No, we couldn't put Mother in here. We might just as well make a place for her to lie down outside in the snow.

I groped my way carefully down the stairs to the cellar. It was pitch-dark, but there was hardly any draught and the snow hadn't sifted down that far. It was noticeably warmer here than upstairs or outside. I felt my way to the corner where I had once seen the three dead children nestled against each other. They weren't there any more. I got the bags from outside and brought them to the cellar. Then I ran back to find my parents.

12

The baby was born that night. It arrived while I was frantically running back and forth in our street, trying to locate the woman who had offered me the embers. But I couldn't remember which house it was, and in the meantime it had become dark. No one would open their doors. They were all afraid of strangers who were so hungry they would stop at nothing, not even murder.

By the time I had groped my way back down into the dark cellar, the baby's umbilical cord had already been cut.

"It's a girl, Roland," I heard Mother say. "We're going to call her Jessica Marta, right, Klaus?"

"Whatever you like, Inge," my father answered.

He sent me off on another errand.

"I took the mattress out of the pram to put your mother on," he said. "It's all bloody now, and there's nothing for the baby to lie on. Go out and see if you can find an armful of hay in any of the barns."

I ran out and searched through the castle barns in the dark. I knew my way around them well. I didn't find any hay, because Judith and Mother had taken it all when the children had been at the castle. But I found a big box that rustled when I shook it. I put my hand in and felt that it was full of styrofoam chips. I thought that they would make a reasonably soft and dry bed for a newborn baby, so I carried the box back to the cellar.

But Mother didn't want us to put the baby in the box.

"It'll freeze there," she whispered weakly. "You'll have to keep it warm if it's going to survive."

Father handed the baby to me. Unwashed, just as it had come into the world, it lay in the folds of Grandmother's down pillow.

"Keep it warm for a while," he said, "then I'll take over."

I unbuttoned my jacket and shirt and pressed the little bundle against my bare chest. Wrapped up in Jens's blanket and Father's thickly-lined hiking jacket, I sat down against the wall and pulled my knees up as high as I could. I held my little sister in my lap and scarcely dared to move. The pillow kept both of us warm. I had trouble keeping awake, but the baby was lying in the hollow between my chest and my legs and couldn't slide out very easily. I was careful to make sure that she wasn't in danger of suffocating.

Every time she cried or moved, I felt warm with joy. I was full of tenderness and wanted to do everything possible so that she would survive. For this tiny helpless baby, born into such misery, I was prepared to beg and steal and loot if necessary.

I pictured the baby looking a lot like Kerstin.

I got very stiff from the cold and from sitting so long. I heard Father moving about near Mother; they were talking softly and she groaned once in a while. Then they both grew quiet and all I could hear was their breathing; they must have fallen asleep next to each other. Father was worn out from all the tension and exertion, and Mother from sheer exhaustion. Soon I fell into a restless half-sleep.

When the baby moved again and startled me out of my sleep, the first broad shafts of morning light were coming in through the windows. The first thing I could make out was my frosty breath; then I saw the words that Andreas had written:

111

Parents be DAMNED!

Their large slanting letters filled half the wall. A part of him was still with us.

I dozed off again. When I woke up the next time, it was much lighter. I could see Father and Mother lying nestled close to each other on the cement floor under the sleeping bags. Mother had on Grandfather's thick pullover. Towels and nappies were strewn all around and everything was covered with blood. There was a puddle on the floor; I couldn't tell if it was frozen or not. Mother was lying with her face towards me. She seemed to be sleeping soundly. Her face had a bluish-white cast.

I suddenly remembered Grandfather's garden house. We could have gone there! It even had an old pot-bellied stove. Why hadn't I thought of that before? In any case, though, we probably wouldn't have been able to make it up the steep hill in the dark with Mother in the pram. Well, this had worked out all right. Now that everything was over, we could still move into the garden house as soon as Mother was able to walk again.

When it was light enough for me to distinguish Grandmother's monogram on the pillow cover, I got so curious that I unfolded the pillow and pushed my jacket away from the baby's head to uncover her tiny face.

I froze. I couldn't even scream. I sat without moving.

My little sister Jessica Marta had no eyes. Where they should have been was skin, nothing but ordinary skin. There was only a nose and a mouth, which searched around my chest wanting to suck.

The horror of it paralysed me so, that I wasn't even able to grab the ends of the pillow when the baby started to kick. There she lay now, naked and bloody, and I saw that she had only stumps for arms.

"Dad," I whispered. "Dad –"

He raised himself on his elbow with a start and blinked at me with reddened eyes. His breath was white.

"Look," I whispered.

"Yes," he said, "I know. She bled to death. She knew it was coming. She died very peacefully; it was a good death. She talked about you at the very end."

But I wasn't focussing on anything but my new sister. I thought he was talking about her.

"She isn't dead," I said, "she's been moving the whole time –"

He crawled over to me and bent over my knee.

"Oh, no, no," he moaned.

Now I looked over at Mother. Slowly the realisation came to me. Then I started to scream. I screamed and screamed until, bathed in sweat, I lost consciousness.

When I came to, I heard the baby crying. Its voice was coming out of the box of styrofoam chips. It was a strong voice. Father was carrying the box over to the stairs.

"Where are you taking it?" I asked fearfully.

"Just go to sleep," he said.

I noticed that he was trying not to look at me.

"But you can't do that," I whispered.

Tears were running down his cheeks.

"Which is the more merciful thing to do?" he said.

I stumbled over to him and put my hand on the box.

"Try not to hurt her, Dad," I sobbed.

Father nodded.

"Stay here," he said. "Stay here with Mother."

He was gone only a short time, but it seemed like hours. When I finally heard his footsteps on the stairs, I went to meet him coming down. He was still holding the box in his hands. But now no crying or rustling noises were coming from it.

On the same day we moved up to Grandfather's garden house. We put Mother back in the pram and covered her up well. There was no one in the streets, no one to ask any questions. With great effort we managed to shove the pram up the icy slope. When the next thaw came, we buried both of them, Mother and Jessica Marta, under the cherry tree.

13

Four years have gone by since then. I'm seventeen now. We lived in Grandfather's garden house for two years, then moved back to the house by the South Gate. Almost half of those who had made it through the first devastating winter died during the second, including Mrs. Kramer and the old man. Only the girl who had been living with them survived. We let her stay with us.

There are quite a few houses in Schevenborn now that are in reasonable shape but standing empty. Of all the townspeople and the refugees who found a place to stay here, only about four hundred remain. No, the others didn't all die. Two years ago a rumour started to circulate, claiming that there were no epidemics or radioactive contamination in the Alps, and that life was going on there as it always had. Hearing that, over a hundred and fifty people got their belongings together and headed south. Up till now, none of them have come back. Maybe the rumour was true, maybe not. My father and I preferred not to know if there was anything to it. We'd already left once and come back crushed. We're staying here. There are places where we would be much worse off. That's been confirmed by a lot of the people who occasionally pass through. "Life is still going on here," they say.

These four years have brought nothing but fear: fear of the cold, of starvation and disease, of insect plagues. Fear of death.

Most of the townspeople who had survived the day of the bomb died during the first two winters that followed the disaster. In the second winter especially, only a small number survived. It was a very cold winter; people froze or starved to death.

It had been very difficult to gather enough food for the approaching winter, because in the year after the explosion almost nothing would grow. Most of the fields were left unsown. Even the people who had been able to plant a few potatoes or some grain ended up with no harvest. The earth was radioactive. The plants that germinated in the spring soon withered away. Instead of its usual fresh green, the landscape wore a coat of sulphurous yellow. Pine trees shed their needles, and the buds on many of the deciduous trees didn't develop. Only the toughest weeds held their own.

During that first summer after the bomb and in the following winter, people ate grass and bark; they gathered roots and choked down caterpillars and worms. They trudged across the country in hope of finding something edible. The remaining cats and dogs were eaten. People even ate rats. It seemed that the bomb hadn't had any effect on them. Clever new ways of trapping them alive were developed, and people bragged back and forth about how many they'd caught. Yes, the townspeople owed their lives to the rats, and to the large supply of canned goods that had been discovered at a subterranean military base near Fulda. Some young people from the town had come upon it by chance and had broken in and ransacked the place.

They had tried in vain to keep this find a secret. All of Schevenborn fought for the cans. Even today the few that are still left are in high demand as items of barter. During the worst periods, people killed to get their hands on them.

But last winter hardly anyone died of starvation in

Schevenborn. Slowly, very slowly, nature is beginning to recover from the enormous assault. Robust growth is making itself evident once more. Last spring we could see green again outside the town. Even over towards the Fulda grass is sprouting out of the ash. It's not the most common kind; only the hardiest varieties can make it. But whatever kind it is, the main thing is that the awful ashen grey is disappearing.

People are planting gardens again. There are lots of varieties of vegetables that you don't see any more; they weren't able to survive the radiation. But there are still potatoes. All around Schevenborn, on the fringes of town, you'll come upon individual beds of potatoes and little fields full of them. During the warm season the townspeople's lives revolve around their potatoes, because the insects have got out of control now that all the birds are dead. We've lived through terrible insect plagues. And a large number of wild boars, hidden away in hollows and protected by dense undergrowth, apparently survived the explosion, too. They've multiplied unbelievably and have been invading the fields in packs. If only we had ammunition!

But the townspeople are getting inventive. This spring and summer, using traps and pits, they caught four wild boars. Every survivor had learned by now that anyone who doesn't build up a stockpile of provisions is risking starvation by next winter at the latest.

There is more land available outside town now than the few remaining inhabitants can make use of. The borders of what was once cultivated land, both gardens and fields, are still visible, and a few fences remain standing around what was once pasture land. But from year to year the traces of the days before the bomb are becoming less distinct.

Money has disappeared, too. Sometimes you will see children playing with coins and bills. But they've become worthless. Anyone who is in urgent need of some item has to trade something else for it. Bartering has become universal. People even exchange labour back and forth. Inventiveness is highly valued and those who have a profession that's more or less unnecessary now try to think of ways they can make use of their talents and hobbies. A few of the more imaginative townspeople are already constructing a new water-supply system. There are certainly enough pipes lying around in the piles of rubble.

Since last winter, when starvation was still rampant, there's been no more looting or killing. A certain amount of order has returned. Corpses that people find in a meadow somewhere, or when they're out gathering wood or picking beechnuts, are given a decent burial. It doesn't matter if no one knows who they were or if there's not much left of them.

Schevenborn even has a mayor again. When something has to be decided, he calls a meeting of the survivors between the mountains of rubble on what used to be Market Square. Hardly a building was left standing there, but the old cobblestone pavement is indestructible.

The people of Schevenborn look like the poor of the Third World now. Many of us are still wearing clothing from before the bomb: washed-out, frayed, patched things. Our shoes are made of old tyres and pieces of wood. A lot of the women have made new clothes out of old rags. We don't really know yet what we'll do for clothes once all the old material is worn out. But we don't let that bother us. For the moment there are more important things to take care of.

We don't keep ourselves as neat and clean as we used to. Bathrooms with running water are non-existent, and there are no barbers or cosmetics. We don't even have soap. We smell sweaty. We smell like work.

Our life is constant toil; otherwise we wouldn't make it through the next winter. Everything has to be done by hand: hauling water and washing clothes and sewing; planting and harvesting; removing rubble and doing construction work. We don't have machines any more.

We have to make the most of the daylight hours. As soon as the sun rises, everyone who still lives in Schevenborn is working, even four- or five-year-old children. Each person has to share in the work so that no one starves or freezes to death. So there's hardly any time left for playing or going on walks. And we're haunted by gnawing fears: Will it be a hard winter? Will we be able to keep insects away from the potatoes? Will we stay healthy? Will we be able to stay alive? It wouldn't take anything more than a case of blood poisoning, or jaundice, or an attack of appendicitis to kill us, because the last doctor is dead and there are no drugs left.

But we all hide our fears; we avoid acknowledging the danger that hangs over us. If we didn't, we'd go crazy. And so our endangered lives are gradually being transformed into ordinary ones, with all their daily routines.

For a good year now we've even had a school again. My father set it up. There are two classes, one for the little children and one for the older ones. Schevenborn without a school was unimaginable to my father. I would say that a cannibal is less shocking to him than an illiterate. When I was younger I thought that way, too. Before the bomb it was a foregone conclusion that everyone should learn reading, writing and arithmetic. In the meantime, though, I've come to believe that education of that sort isn't the most important thing in our current situation.

At first we had forty-nine pupils from six to fourteen. The little ones are my responsibility, while Father teaches the older group. He does the three Rs with his pupils, but he never talks to them about the bomb, or compares the way things were before with how they are now. Recently he taught them a little about the ancient Greeks. But that was about the extent of it. What he teaches them best is how to add quickly in their heads and how to spell. There's no hiding the fact that he was once a book-keeper. But who needs book-keepers these days?

The parents give us what they can in payment for our teaching: a few potatoes, sunflower seeds, canned food. Children whose parents have nothing bring us wood from the forest.

My father really puts in a lot of effort. He looks through the heaps of rubble and old rubbish dumps to try to find paper and writing utensils for the pupils. Since they're so valuable, he watches over the pens and pencils that he lends to the children every day. They simply must not be wasted or lost. The supplies from before the bomb have to be used as sparingly as possible, since they're irreplaceable. What will happen when they're gone? We don't know. But we do know that we can't manufacture paper or pencils, to say nothing of ballpoint pens.

We don't do our teaching in either of the former school buildings. The primary school burned down a year after the bomb when lightning started a fire. And the other school, which had been built not long before, consisted of nothing but a skeleton of walls after all the window panes had been smashed and the roof blown off.

So we set up two classrooms on the main floor of the castle. It's protected from the wind by high trees, has thick walls, and the roof and ceiling are still intact. We walled up the windows halfway; if it gets too stormy, we shove a couple of big old cabinets in front of them. There's a pot-bellied stove in each room, but on the coldest days we cancel classes.

The townspeople helped us clean the two rooms; they were happy that there was going to be a school for their children again. They tried to help my father wash Andreas's writing off the walls, but it wouldn't come off, neither inside nor on the outer walls. It's still legible in the cellar, too. But I don't like to go down there; it brings back too many memories.

The rats are the only real problem. The castle is full of them. They run between the pupils' feet during lessons. All of Schevenborn is suffering from this plague of rats. And of course there aren't any cats left. Whenever you walk through the streets you see rats flitting past. From year to year they multiply, getting fatter and more aggressive. Not even the second winter wiped them out, when starving townspeople began to eat rat meat in order to survive. Recently a barefoot seven-year-old was bitten on the toe, and now all the other children are frightened and sit on their legs in class. How are we supposed to teach when they have to worry about such things?

Fear, never-ending fear. As if our pupils didn't have enough to be afraid of already. Many of them aren't from Schevenborn; they were from the Fulda area and ended up here after the explosion. Many are orphans. The younger ones can hardly remember their parents. Some of them walk on crutches, others are covered with scars. In my class there are two blind pupils. One of my father's is a mute; he's missing part of his tongue. Several have no hair, others suffer from seizures. Many of them come to school tired, because they're tormented by nightmares. Scarcely any of our pupils are physically and mentally sound. We have to be careful what we say to them, otherwise they burst into tears.

But they're alive. They've survived. And so have I. Whenever I think about that, it seems incomprehensible to me, since there's only one survivor for every twenty who have died.

Have we survived? Will it be my turn next? Today I noticed that more hair than usual was left in my comb. That's the way it started with Judith, too.

Although children have been born after the bomb, the population is still decreasing. Many people don't want to bear the responsibility of bringing children into this devastated world. I've heard of women who have become infertile since the explosion. And there are still frequent cases of radiation sickness.

"It'll be with us for a long time," my father said. "It's even lying in wait for the children who haven't been born yet."

At first I didn't want to accept that. Jessica Marta – in her case it was understandable because she'd already been conceived when the radiation struck. But all those children who weren't conceived until *after* the explosion – how could they possibly have been affected as well?

"Congenital defects," my father said.

Hardly any of the newborn babies around Schevenborn are normal. Almost all of those born alive are crippled or blind, deaf-mutes or imbeciles. They destroy every last hope we have, because no matter how hard the townspeople try to survive, it's clear that they'll die off, too. It's only a question of time.

My father has changed a lot since the bomb. He doesn't talk much any more. Shortly after he opened the school, a boy with a scarred face threw a piece of chalk at him and screamed, "You murderer!" Later the boy died a horrible death brought on by radiation sickness.

The other children had looked at the boy in horror, but my father had known right away what he meant. Ever since then he hasn't slept well. I often hear him moaning during the night. Sometimes he looks at me as if he were expecting me to call him a murderer, too.

But what would it change if I were to accuse him, along with almost everyone else in his generation, of simply looking on while others were preparing the annihilation of mankind? Or of always giving the lame excuse, "How can *we* do anything to change it?" and pointing out that such fearful weapons guaranteed peace, precisely because they were so terrible? Or of wanting comfort and prosperity more than anything else?

Once a girl in his class asked him, "Did *you* do anything for peace?"

He only shook his head. But at least I could respect his honesty.

The older I get and the more I ponder this whole matter, the more I have to agree with Andreas: Parents be damned! But I would add to that: Grandparents be damned! They should have known what demons were being conjured up, because they'd had the experience of war – even though their war was nothing compared to our day of the bomb.

Now we have forty children in our school. By the end of the year there will be only thirty-seven, because radiation sickness has struck three more: the Kernmeyers' son, Uli, the brightest one in my class and the last survivor of four brothers and sisters; a first-grader named Berti, who was brought to Schevenborn from the meadows near Fulda and who doesn't know who his parents are or what his last name is; and our little Barbel, the girl who had stayed with Mrs. Kramer. She's been with us for two years now and has become a member of the family. It will be hard for us to see her die.

We'll be closing one of the classes soon.

"You can take over the pupils who are left," my father said to me yesterday. When I gave him a surprised look, he added, "They won't call you a murderer."

Yes, I'll take over the class. I like teaching. Of course, I'm still too young to be a teacher, and I've never really learned how. But the children will accept me because I wasn't a grown-up when the bomb was dropped.

There are so many things more important than reading, writing and arithmetic that I absolutely have to teach them: they must want a life without looting, stealing, and killing. They must learn to respect each other again, and to give help where help is needed. They must learn to talk with each other and work together to find solutions to their problems, instead of immediately striking out at one another. They must feel responsible for each other. They must love each other. Their world must become a peaceful one – even though it will not last long.

For these are the last children of Schevenborn.

EPILOGUE

There can hardly be any doubt that our very existence is being threatened by the steadily growing number of nuclear weapons. But many people put this threat out of their minds and refuse to think about it. They consider the annihilation of the human race to be unimaginable.

I have tried to make it imaginable through this story. It is extremely difficult to portray future events for which there are no precedents; such portrayals are open to debate, and one can conceive of several different variations. I have depicted the disaster and its consequences as less catastrophic than they presumably would be in reality, since I had to allow for a survivor who would later be in a position to talk about what had happened.

Perhaps my story will encourage all of us to begin to resist the threat of a nuclear holocaust. It is still not too late!

GUDRUN PAUSEWANG

TIME PIPER

Delia Huddy

"The door of the lab burst open. Something came out; something at floor level. It was lucky that Luke was not in the corridor or he might have been knocked out... Whatever it was came from the laboratory in a living torrent of bodies and swept down the corridor."

From the day he meets the beautiful, remote mysterious Hare, Luke's life is turned upside down. But what can be the connection between this strange lost girl and Tom Humboldt the brilliant inventor of a Time Machine? The answer, it seems, lies in the past...

"Very ingenious... A very good book."
The Standard

"Very perceptive ... not really sci-fi but a love story."
Peter Hunt
The Times Literary Supplement

SO MUCH TO TELL YOU
John Marsden

Scarred by her past, Marina has withdrawn into a silence. But then, set the task of writing a journal by her English teacher, she finds a new outlet for her thoughts and feelings and for exploring the traumatic events which have caused her distress.

"Beautifully written... A splendid read."
The Times Educational Supplement

Australian Book of the Year (Older Fiction) 1988

DOUBLE VISION

Diana Hendry

"People would do a lot better if they could see double like me... I mean seeing things two ways – with the head and the heart. Reason and imagination."

It's the 1950s and, for fifteen-year-old Eliza Bishop, life in a small, North West coastal town is unbearably claustrophobic. But for her small, fearful sister Lily, the seaside setting affords unlimited scope to her imaginative mind. Through these two very different pairs of eyes a memorable range of characters, events and emotions is brought into vision.

"Succeeds totally where very few books do, as a novel which bestrides the two worlds of adult and children's fiction with total success in both... The stuff of which the very best fiction is wrought."
Susan Hill, The Sunday Times

"Full of acute observation and humour."
Geoffrey Trease,
The Times Educational Supplement

MORE WALKER PAPERBACKS
For You to Enjoy

☐ 0-7445-0849-5   *Through the Dolls'*
House Door   £2.99
by Jane Gardam

☐ 0-7445-1435-5   *Sweet Whispers,*
Brother Rush   £2.99
by Virginia Hamilton

☐ 0-7445-1313-8   *The Silent Shore*   £2.99
by Ruth Elwin Harris

☐ 0-7445-1356-1   *The Beckoning Hills*   £2.99
by Ruth Elwin Harris

☐ 0-7445-2066-5   *Second Star to*
the Right   £2.99
by Deborah Hautzig

☐ 0-7445-2044-4   *Double Vision*   £2.99
by Diana Hendry

☐ 0-7445-1478-9   *Time Piper*   £2.99
by Delia Huddy

☐ 0-7445-1449-5   *So Much To Tell You*   £2.99
by John Marsden

**Walker Paperbacks are available from most booksellers. They are also available
by post: just tick the titles you want, fill in the form below and send it to
Walker Books Ltd, PO Box 11, Falmouth, Cornwall TR10 9EN.**

Please send a cheque or postal order and allow the following for postage and packing:
UK & BFPO – £1.00 for first book, plus 50p for second book and
plus 30p for each additional book to a maximum charge of £3.00
Overseas and Eire Custo...
plus ...
Prices are correct at time ...

Name _____

Address _____

_____